Memories of the London Theatre 1900–1914

by
ALLAN WADE

Edited by
ALAN ANDREWS

The Society for Theatre Research
1983

Published by The Society for Theatre Research
77 Kinnerton Street, London SW1X 8ED

ISBN 0 85430 037 6

Printed in Great Britain at The Pitman Press, Bath

Contents

FOREWORD   by George Speaight   v

CONSTANCE KYRLE FLETCHER: A TRIBUTE   by Norman Philbrick   vi

EDITOR'S INTRODUCTION   vii

ACKNOWLEDGEMENTS   ix

MEMORIES OF THE LONDON THEATRE   1

APPENDIX   37

ALLAN WADE'S LATER YEARS   39

NOTES   44

A PERSONAL MEMORY   by Freda Gaye   48

INDEX   51

Illustrations

between pages 22 and 23

1 Pencil sketch of Allan Wade
2 Granville Barker and Madge McIntosh in *Mrs. Warren's Profession*
3 Sketch of J. E. Vedrenne
4 Arthur Symons
5 Henry Ainley in Barker's *Twelfth Night*
6 Lillah McCarthy in Barker's *The Winter's Tale*
7 The fairy court in Barker's *A Midsummer Night's Dream*
8 Wish Wynne in *The Great Adventure*

on page 20

The programme for the copyright performance of *Waste*

The illustration on plate 1 is reproduced by courtesy of Mrs. Peggy Wade; those on plates 3, 4, 5, 6 and 8 by courtesy of The Raymond Mander & Joe Mitchenson Theatre Collection; and those on plates 2 and 7 and on page 20 by courtesy of The Theatre Museum at the Victoria & Albert Museum.

Foreword

This volume serves a double purpose. Firstly, it completes the programme planned for the Society's 1982/3 publication year, from which Eric Walter White's *Register of First Performances of English Operas* has already appeared. And secondly, it enables the Society to offer a fitting memorial to the memory of one of its earliest supporters.

Constance Kyrle Fletcher was a gifted amateur actress as a member of the Newport Playgoers Society. After her marriage she became a partner in her husband's antiquarian theatrical bookselling firm, when it was established in London, where she specialized in the manuscript side of the business. She continued to carry this on after her husband's death. She had long been involved in theatre history as a friend and executor of Gabriele Enthoven, founder of the Enthoven Collection at the Victoria and Albert Museum. So it was fitting that she took an active part in the formation of The Society for Theatre Research and was hostess at the very first meeting at her house in Wimbledon at which the idea of such a society was mooted. After the death of Ifan Kyrle Fletcher she succeeded him as a valued member of its committee.

After her death in 1980 a number of her friends expressed a wish to honour her memory in some way, and a fund was opened for this purpose. To this fund has been added a generous bequest left to the Society in her will. Professor Norman Philbrick's tribute expresses the feelings of many who wished to associate themselves with this memorial.

In considering how best to give expression to the wishes of those who contributed to the Constance Kyrle Fletcher Memorial Fund, the committee of the Society has had two aims in view. These were that the memorial should advance the study of theatre history; and that it should, in some way, reflect Constance's interest in theatrical manuscripts. It was at this point that our attention was drawn to the manuscript of the uncompleted memoirs of Allan Wade, who had played an important part as spectator and behind the scenes in the theatrical life of Britain in the early decades of the twentieth century, just at the time when Constance was herself entering upon her life-long involvement with the stage.

It has therefore seemed fitting to publish these Memoirs, both for their own considerable interest and as a suitable memorial to Constance Kyrle Fletcher. We must express our thanks to Sir Rupert Hart-Davis, Allan Wade's literary executor, for facilitating the printing of his Memoirs; to Mrs. Peggy Wade for providing the portrait of him reproduced here; to Miss Freda Gaye for researching other illustrations; and to Professor Alan Andrews, who first drew our attention to this manuscript and who has edited it for publication.

George Speaight
Chairman Publications Committee
The Society for Theatre Research

Constance Kyrle Fletcher
A Tribute

Although we, the members of The Society for Theatre Research, labour to foster dedication to the theatre and its manifold arts, there are many who make silent yet incalculable contribution without which the theatre could not be the fabulous source of inspiration and growth it is. One of these labourers was Constance Kyrle Fletcher. She was tireless in her support of the drama and theatre. With her sound judgment, her vast knowledge of theatre arts, her keen interest in all those who wrote about the theatre or who were strongly active in its creative and practical work, and her objective observation of those who bring joy to others through art, Constance Fletcher was an ever-present source of encouragement to all of us.

Norman and Geraldine Philbrick

Introduction

In 1979, in the course of extensive research into the history of the Stage Society, I wrote to Sir Rupert Hart-Davis to see if he knew whether there were any surviving papers of Allan Wade and if so where they might be. I had come across Wade's name several times, as actor in plays produced by the Society, as director of productions, as the Secretary of the Society and as a translator of two plays. I knew he had contributed an essay, "Shaw and the Stage Society," to Mander and Mitchenson's *Theatrical Companion to Shaw*; and also that he had edited Yeats's letters and Henry James's writings on the theatre and had been involved in transcribing Max Beerbohm's uncollected theatre reviews for publication. Since all of these latter items had been published by Rupert Hart-Davis, it seemed logical to approach him.

Sir Rupert promptly replied that he had Allan Wade's papers. Subsequently he invited me to visit him and look at what there was. In the main, the collection seemed to comprise letters to Wade in connection with the edition of Yeats's letters with some concerning the edition of Oscar Wilde's letters which Sir Rupert had himself edited after Wade's death. There were some other memorabilia, and an absorbing manuscript of ninety pages or so in which Wade recalled the theatre as he had known it in the early years of this century.

Unfortunately for my immediate interest, the manuscript came to an end just at the point at which Wade became Secretary of the Stage Society. However, it was obviously such an interesting document in itself as to warrant publication for a larger readership. Wade had been Granville Barker's secretary and assistant at the Court Theatre and after, had been in touch with major figures, in the theatre and literature during the years before the First World War, and besides this was himself a writer of great charm.

I discussed the possibility of publication with several people. Of these the most enthusiastic was Miss Freda Gaye, who had herself known Allan Wade well, having acted under his direction in the nineteen-twenties. Eventually, thanks also to the encouragement of Jack Reading, the Society for Theatre Research decided that it would publish the memoir.

Allan Wade was born on 17 May 1881, the son of the Rev. Stephen Wade of Boscastle in Cornwall. He was educated at Blundell's School in Tiverton. When he came to London at the turn of the century he was, as he says in these memoirs, destined for a career in business. But he also tells us how he extricated himself from this fate, and instead set about making a life in the theatre and in letters.

Wade seems to have been inhibited from pursuing a theatrical career so long as his father was alive but soon after the rector of Boscastle died, Allan Wade made his first appearance on the stage. This took place at the Crown Theatre, Peckham, on 1 August 1904 in a melodrama entitled *A Daughter's Crime*. Later in 1904, he joined F. R. Benson's B Company, also known as Benson North. His most important part appears to have been Gratiano in *The Merchant of Venice* but he was sufficiently impressive in that for one reporter to comment that he was supported by the actor playing Bassanio. Playing Nerissa opposite him, and several other leading female roles, was Katherine Boyce. She later became the wife of General George C. Marshall, U.S. Secretary of State from 1947 to 1949. It is from Wade's reference to this that we can give an approximate date to his manuscript.

Wade left the Benson tour at the end of the 1904–1905 season and was engaged by the Vedrenne–Barker management at the Court Theatre. He soon became Granville Barker's secretary and assistant, and so was in a privileged position to observe the events of those years. Generally he understudied, but occasionally he was given a part such as Ferrers in Cyril Harcourt's *The Reformer* and Callow in the Housman–Barker fantasy, *Prunella*. Wade remained with the Vedrenne–Barker management when it removed to the Savoy and the Haymarket in 1907, and he then became play-reader and assistant to Barker for the Frohman repertory season at the Duke of York's in 1909–1910. He also acted as agent for the Irish Players in London in 1909. Wade returned to work for Barker again as play-reader when, together with Lillah McCarthy, Barker took over the Little Theatre in 1911, and then the Kingsway in 1912. The Barkers remained lessees of the Kingsway until January 1915.

By this time Wade had developed many of the interests in literature which would stay with him throughout his life. In particular, he had begun collecting Yeats, and this led to the bibliography which was published in 1908. Yeats was only one of Wade's literary friends and acquaintances. Others were Conrad, Galsworthy, Bennett, George Moore, and of course Shaw. He was clearly devoted to Granville Barker and he also greatly admired Gordon Craig, whose sister Edith he knew quite well.

These memoirs come to a halt in 1911 when Wade became Secretary of the Incorporated Stage Society. Important work on his own account was still to come, especially with the Phoenix Society in the 1920s, in his continuing association with the Stage Society and in the literary work which he took up when his active theatre days were over. It has therefore been felt appropriate to add some information about his later career at the end of his memoir.

Acknowledgements

My thanks are principally due to Sir Rupert Hart-Davis for his kindness in giving me access to the Wade papers in the first place, for his conversation, and to him and his wife, June, for their hospitality to myself and my family. I am also grateful to Freda Gaye for sharing with me her memories of Wade and vigorously encouraging the publication of these memoirs by the Society for Theatre Research. Jack Reading, a friend of many years, was also encouraging, and George Speaight has been a patient and courteous editor on behalf of the Society. I must also acknowledge the assistance of Dean K. T. Leffek and the Research Development Fund at Dalhousie University for a research grant which enabled me to verify and clarify factual matters through investigations at the British Library and to examine the letters to Wade from W. B. Yeats which are in the Lilly Library at Indiana University. My wife, Katherine, helped me by suggesting the kinds of thing that needed amplification and what might make interesting illustrations. Finally, I thank Kathleen Barker, who made a typescript of the original manuscript, and Janet Jacques for additional typing.

Alan Andrews
Dalhousie University,
Halifax, Canada.
31 May 1983

I

To review my memories of the London theatre as I first knew it, in the very early days of this century, is to recall a period of great prosperity and of some considerable achievement. This was the era of the actor-manager. Although Irving's long reign at the Lyceum was nearing its end—his farewell performances there were given in July of 1902—the tradition of grandiose and ornate productions of Shakespeare had been taken over by Beerbohm Tree at His Majesty's Theatre. At the St. James's George Alexander was giving well-groomed performances of modern comedy varied with an occasional "costume" play; Charles Wyndham was to be found at one or other of the three theatres he controlled, the Criterion, Wyndham's or the New; Cyril Maude kept the Haymarket's tradition for comedy at a high level, Arthur Bourchier exploited his own talent and that of his wife Violet Vanbrugh at the Garrick. Other actor-managers divided their time between London and the provinces, having no theatre permanently under their control but playing a London season as occasion demanded; these included John Hare, Forbes-Robertson, Fred Terry and Julia Neilson, Mrs. Patrick Campbell, Martin Harvey; even the Kendals, though their date for retirement was not far off,[1] now and then brought a play to London.

Although it was not unusual, both at that time and later, to decry the actor-manager and to consider his influence on dramatic art a baneful one, there was, none the less, much to be said in his favour. He was, to begin with, in almost every case, "a man of the theatre", that is he had been an actor from his earliest days and had faced the usual struggles and disappointments which then were the almost inevitable accompaniment of a stage career. In nearly every case they had made for themselves a position of some eminence before going into management, and although, having acquired theatres, the plays they produced were selected usually because they contained showy parts for the manager and his leading actress, they could reasonably argue that it was to see them in such parts that the public was ready to pay money at the doors. Nor did they rely wholly on their own merits; both Tree and Alexander especially took care to surround themselves with good players for the subsidiary parts. Great care and much money were expended in the mounting of plays; everything at His Majesty's was on a very sumptuous scale—Tree, indeed, was sometimes considered to have smothered Shakespeare's poetry with gorgeous accessories.

There were, of course, many other theatres and their managements; some of them produced farce, some melodrama. At the Gaiety and at Daly's George Edwardes produced that particularly English form of entertainment then called musical comedy. It was well named for the scores were musical and the comedians were funny. There were music halls too; at some, such as the Tivoli, the Pavilion and the Oxford, the programme consisted of a series of "turns', while at the Empire and the Alhambra, the second half of the programme offered patrons a gorgeous spectacular ballet, lasting perhaps an hour and a half. These ballets were probably, in their time, unique in Europe. Nor was this all; for every summer, when the theatre season in Paris was over, leading French actors and actresses paid a short visit to London; Sarah Bernhardt came almost every year, Coquelin, Réjane, Jane Hading, Jeanne Granier. Duse also appeared in a series of performances and there was a couple of visits of a Japanese company headed by the actress Sada Yacco and her husband Kawakami.[2] American actors did not visit in great numbers, but William Gillette brought his play on Sherlock Holmes to the Lyceum in

1

1901, and I can remember a production of Augustus Thomas's drama *Arizona* at the Adelphi in the following year, in which London was much impressed by the smoothness of ensemble and the brisk pace of the acting.

Such, then, was the kind of theatre I first knew. I had spent my early days in the West of England and my visits to London had hitherto been few and brief. Now I was able to indulge my passion for the theatre as much as I could desire, and I set myself, almost formally, to explore English acting and drama. I had read plays as far back as I can remember; anything written in dialogue form, even if not intended for the stage, I visualized as though it was taking place before my eyes on the boards of a theatre. In a year or two I was so familiar with the insides of the London theatres that had I been blindfolded and put down in the auditorium of any of them I believe that, on removal of the bandage, I should have been able to name the theatre I was in, from its interior architecture and decoration. The modern theatre is not so easily identifiable; a barn-like uniformity seems the mark of recent playhouse architecture.[3]

Playgoing was an agreeable pursuit in those bygone days. In the stalls and dress circle evening dress was the almost invariable custom; prices, of course, were lower than they have since become and in the best theatres no charge was made for a programme or for the custody of one's hat and coat. Even the smaller theatres had orchestras. And one was given good value for one's money; unless the play was exceptionally long, the earlier arrivals in pit and gallery were entertained with a curtain-raiser, while those occupants of booked seats who cared to finish their dinners at leisure could still arrive in time for the principal entertainment. The final curtain fell usually about eleven o'clock or a little later, which left one ample time for supper, "closing time" in those Arcadian days being fixed at half an hour past midnight.

It was, I suppose, because London's theatres were so much a novelty to me that I do not remember being very critical of the quality of the plays I saw, in spite of the fact that I was well enough acquainted with such "advanced" drama as was then in print. I must have taken it for granted that one could not expect to see these tender plants exposed to the ordeal of performance at a West End theatre. For just as the leading managements went to the best tailors and dressmakers for the clothing of their performers and to the best realistic scene painters for their stage decoration, so they applied to the most successful practitioners of dramatic writing for the plays they performed. A. W. Pinero and Henry Arthur Jones had, in the previous decade, established themselves as the two foremost English playwrights; opinion was divided as to which was the greater. Pinero usually now took a year and sometimes two over each new play, and had more successes than failures; Henry Arthur Jones had a higher percentage of failure but was rather more prolific. These two were closely followed in popularity by R. C. Carton and Haddon Chambers; J. M. Barrie was beginning to make his mark but his big successes were yet to come. There were younger men also such as Alfred Sutro and Hubert Henry Davies who were beginning to discover just how to turn out the marketable play which would fit some particular popular stage figure and please his or her public. And there were others; Cecil Raleigh was generally ready with a new and topical melodrama for Drury Lane each autumn, and Stephen Phillips, who had been a Shakespearean actor, produced a series of verse plays the earliest of which seemed at the time to mark the beginning of a rebirth of poetic drama. *Herod* at His Majesty's in 1900, *Paolo and Francesca* at the St. James's in 1902 (but accepted earlier) and *Ulysses* at His Majesty's in the same year all gave opportunities for elaborate and picturesque mounting and provided plenty of opportunity for good acting. But his later plays were not very successful and in spite of one or two other valiant attempts such as the *Attila* of Laurence Binyon,[4] poetry (except for Shakespeare) vanished almost entirely from the London stage. The comfortable theatre-going public, however, seemed entirely satisfied with the entertainment it was given. There had been, during the nineties, some attempts to induce it to take some interest in what was considered a more advanced drama, but that had had very little effect. Ibsen was now regarded rather in the way that in recent days, we have looked at a bomb or land mine which has been "dealt with" and rendered harmless; there had been a time when his plays might have been devastatingly dangerous but that was, somehow, happily passed. People were aware of Bernard Shaw as the man who used to write so amusingly about plays in the *Saturday Review* and, before that, so amusingly about music in the *World*. He had published a couple of volumes of plays, to which he had recently added a third, and those were very amusing too—to read. The thought that they might be acted did not seem to occur to anybody. Yet a few of them had been performed. *Widowers' Houses* had been played once as far back as 1892 and *Arms and the Man* had had a *succès de scandale* at the Avenue in 1894, playing for about six weeks to poor houses. *The Devil's Disciple*, taken on tour by an actor named Murray Carson, reached the London suburbs in 1899. But Irving had not seen himself either as the young Napoleon in *The Man of Destiny* nor as Captain Brassbound in the play Shaw had written for Ellen Terry, and Charles Wyndham didn't want to appear as the clergyman-husband of Candida; nor did William Terriss find occasion to use *The Devil's Disciple* which was written at his instigation. Strangest of all, the Haymarket Theatre actually put *You Never Can Tell* in rehearsal and then, for reasons which still remain obscure, in spite of the amusing account of the episode which Bernard Shaw contributed, anonymously, to Cyril Maude's *History of the Haymarket Theatre*,[5] the play was shelved.

When I wrote above that the thought of performing Shaw's plays did not occur "to anybody", I must qualify this by explaining that I meant to anybody who was managing a theatre for the public. There was a private society, to which I shall presently come, where the performance of Shaw's plays was undertaken with much vigour, and with, eventually, far-reaching effect. This was known as the Stage Society.

II

In the spring of 1901 somebody said to me casually, "You should see the revival at Wyndham's Theatre of *The Case of Rebellious Susan*; I hear that Granville Barker gives a remarkable performance." The name of this actor was not quite unknown to me for I remembered reading an appreciative review signed St. J. H. in the *Academy* of a play called *The Weather Hen*[6] of which he had been part author; it had been produced at a special matinee in June, 1899 at Terry's Theatre and was given a few more performances at the Comedy in the following month. So I lost no time in booking a seat at Wyndham's for H. A. Jones's play, and found that my informant had, if anything, understated the case. Not long ago I read this play to make sure that my memory had not failed me, and was surprised to discover that here had been a case in which the art of the actor had indeed made dry bones live. The character, called Fergusson Pybus, a pompously silly young man whose desire it is to "stamp himself on the age" in some unspecified manner, is drawn conventionally and written without wit and with a rather commonplace sense of fun; Barker made this lay figure a living individual and played in a spirit of high comedy. Where the other characters and their performance have completely faded from my memory, his remains to this day as sharply impressed there as though I had visited the theatre last week. In the autumn of this same year he appeared in *Becky Sharp*,[7] an adaptation of *Vanity Fair* made for Marie Tempest by her husband, Cosmo Gordon Lennox, and Robert Hichens. This time he played a small part, Mr. Wenham, but small as it was he made it unforgettable. There was a scene in which Rawdon Crawley, arrested for debt, is detained in the sponging-house. Expecting his release immediately, it falls to Wenham to tell him he is to be kept there over the week-end. Barker did this with amazing effect. Moving up a wide circular staircase at the back of the scene as he spoke (and actors will know what a difficult business this can be), he delivered poor Rawdon's sentence, "I'm afraid you must make up your mind to stay where you are—till Monday," with a deadly combination of malice and condolence that, again, I have found unforgettable even though nearly half a century has intervened. So impressed had I been that, possibly in the following year, I made a special journey to some suburban theatre where, for a week, Olga Nethersole was playing in a version of Daudet's *Sapho*, made for her by the American dramatist Clyde Fitch, with Granville Barker in the chief male part, Jean.[8] This, however, was a disappointment; the part did not suit him and he could make little of it. But meanwhile I had encountered another facet of his talent, that of the playwright.

About the middle of the year 1899 a small group of people which included Janet Achurch, famous for her pioneer work in Ibsen's plays, Charles Charrington her husband, Walter Crane, Grant Richards, the publisher of Shaw's *Plays Pleasant and Unpleasant*, William Sharp, already making a second literary reputation as the mysterious "Fiona Macleod", and Frederick Whelen, at that time occupying a post in the Bank of England, convened a meeting of about 150 persons known to be interested in dramatic art. Of these some 40 attended, and it was agreed to form a private society for the production of plays which were unlikely to be given by any of the established theatre managements. Membership of the Stage Society, as it was called, was limited to 300, and before the end of the year the first production, Shaw's *You Never Can Tell*, was made at the Royalty Theatre. So that the services of professional performers might be obtained, the performance took place on a Sunday evening, a proceeding then unheard of in London, and one which caused considerable nervousness to the theatre lessees, even though the performance was given for members of a private club. Indeed the difficulty was only met by an understanding that there should be no publicity, and those members of the Society who happened to be dramatic critics were specially asked to make no reports in the Press. It is told that at the first performance representatives of the police arrived to question the legality of even a private performance in a theatre on Sunday, and were adroitly involved in a long argument by Mr. Whelen and others which lasted until the performance had finished.

The cast of this newly formed society's first production was sufficiently remarkable. That brilliant comedian James Welch (who had already appeared in Shaw's earlier plays, *Widowers' Houses* and *Arms and the Man*) directed the production and himself undertook the part of the Waiter; Yorke Stephens, the Bluntschli of *Arms and the Man*, played Valentine and the veteran actor Hermann Vezin appeared as the surly father, Crampton. And the minute and silent *rôle* of Jo, the chef's assistant was taken by the future dramatist, Edward Knoblock.

I am not sure whether Granville Barker had ever appeared under the Charringtons' management, but they certainly knew of his work, and he appears in the cast of the Society's third production, Ibsen's *League of Youth*,[9] which Charrington directed, and was then himself entrusted with the direction of the fourth programme.[10] This was a triple bill: Fiona Macleod's *House of Usna*, (which many years later formed the libretto of Rutland Boughton's music-drama *The Immortal Hour*), and two of Maeterlinck's early plays, *Interior* and *The Death of Tintagiles*. A stray newspaper cutting which has survived among my papers records that in the audience was W. B. Yeats who was heard to say that he could not stand the last act of *Tintagiles* and fled into the street.[11]

Barker appeared again in the next production, Hauptmann's *Coming of Peace*,[12] and Bernard Shaw has recorded how this performance convinced him that the right actor had been found to play Marchbanks, the poet in *Candida*. "His performance," Mr. Shaw says, "was, humanly speaking, perfect."[13]

With the production of *Candida* the Stage Society's first season was brought to a triumphant close. For the next season it was found necessary to increase the limit of membership to 500, to give an additional matinée performance of each play on a week day, and, in the interest of the players who gave their services for nothing, to invite the Press to attend.

It was doubtless because I had read some press notices of these performances that I became fired with a desire to become a member of the Stage Society, and happening to meet one day at a friendly house a brother of Frederick Whelen, the originator of the Society, I asked him to propose me for membership. The third season, due to begin soon after I was enrolled, ran into difficult waters. Greatly daring, the Society announced its intention of performing Bernard Shaw's *Mrs. Warren's Profession*, which had been refused a license by the Lord Chamberlain. Announced for a date early in December 1901, the manager whose theatre had been promised withdrew his permission on hearing that the play was unlicensed. Application was then made successively to twelve theatres, two Music Halls, three Hotels and two Picture Galleries, but in each case, after hopes of success had been raised in some cases, no arrangement could be made. Finally a very small stage was secured at the New Lyric Club (no longer existing) in Coventry Street, and tickets and programmes, which had been several times reprinted, were issued to the Society's members for January 5 and 6, 1902.

In spite of the minute proportions of the stage and preposterous scenery, the play was brilliantly acted, Fanny Brough, an admirable *comédienne* of incisive style, giving a really superb performance of Mrs. Warren, while the part of Frank, the amoral clergyman's son, offered Granville Barker every opportunity to display that impish sense of humour which was so large a part of his charm.

In spite of the discomfort of the auditorium—the floor, I remember, was not raked and the audience sat on bentwood chairs; a part of the time Janet Achurch who was seated immediately in front of me rested one back leg of her chair on my toe!—the play made an immense impression and the author, appearing at the end in his tweed suit with bristling rufous beard, made a speech which I regret to have forgotten. This was the first time I had set eyes on a figure which was later to become so familiar to me. Soon afterwards Grant Richards published a special edition of the play with a new preface by Shaw and illustrations of the performers from photographs taken by F. H. Evans, a city bookseller turned enthusiastic amateur photographer. In his preface Shaw said of this performance: "It is not often that an author . . . is able to step on the stage and apply the strong word genius to the representation with the certainty of eliciting an instant and overwhelming assent from the audience."

A long detour has led me at last to my first encounter with Granville Barker as dramatist. Three weeks after *Mrs. Warren's Profession* came the next Stage Society production, *The Marrying of Ann Leete* at the Royalty Theatre. It is difficult at this time of day to describe the extraordinary effect of novelty which the dialogue of this play conveyed at a first hearing. It was taut, abrupt at times almost monosyllabic, yet gave the impression of looseness, of lack of direction. People answered, not the remark just made to them, but perhaps the last but two or three. Arthur Symons said in his acute criticism of the play, "Mr. Barker can write: he writes in short, sharp sentences, which go off like pistol-shots, and he keeps up the firing, from every corner of the stage."[14] Only the plays of Chekhov, at that time unheard of in the English-speaking theatre, give us the same impression of people pursuing their own trains of thought while the action of the play goes on without regarding them. The play's period is the late 18th Century and the scene mostly in an English country house. In performance it seemed to me that some of the contents, particularly the political implications in the play, were lost; and even in reading it these do not seem to me to be made sufficiently clear. But it is odd that, in later days when experimental theatres have abounded, no revival of the play has, to my knowledge been attempted.[15] A generation which took *The Cherry Orchard* to its bosom might, one would think, have found a welcome for *Ann Leete*—which Bernard Shaw has somewhere called the first of the Heartbreak Houses. I think the Stage Society audience of January 1902 was puzzled and a little resentful. After Ibsen, Shaw and Hauptmann here was something in a very different key—it was no "social drama" in the sense they were accustomed to use those words; it exposed no shocking state of affairs and preached no gospel of reform. But it dealt very humanly—if a little at arm's length—with human men and women in a world that somehow puzzled them and made them a little uneasy and with actions that culminated, suddenly and surprisingly, in Ann Leete's determination to cut herself free of her surroundings. She asks her father's gardener to marry her, and the last scene shows her arriving on her wedding night, tired and rather frightened, at the cottage where she is to live with him. He shows her his few possessions, they say a few words to each other, he timid, she resolute to endure the life she has chosen—and presently they mount the stairs. It is a remarkable piece of dramatic writing, in which emotion is conveyed by the sparsest use of words, and, as I recall, it was beautifully played by Winifred Fraser and C. M. Hallard. The author had directed his own play and already it was clear that he was able to get from his actors the utmost that it was in them to give.

Although produced in 1902 the printed text of the play bears the date 1899, three years earlier. Probably, then, the collaboration with Berte Thomas (whom I remember as a gentle and by no means unaccomplished actor) which had resulted in *The Weather-Hen*, was of an even earlier date. There was another play of this collaboration which bore the odd title *Our Visitor to "Work-a-Day,"* but so far as I can discover it never reached the stage.[16]

Another early work, this time written by Granville Barker alone, was a little one-act play, rather Maeterlinckian in spirit; its title was *A Miracle* and it was described by the author as "an experiment in Dramatic metre" and dated 1900. In 1907 this was given a single performance by the Literary Theatre Society, in a double programme with *The Persians* of Aeschylus.[17] The costumes and scenery for both plays were designed by Charles Ricketts, and *A Miracle* which, as I remember, had two women characters only, was played by Winifred Fraser (Ann Leete) and Gwendolen Bishop with much charm and delicacy.

The year 1902 is memorable to me also for another theatre-going adventure: this was my first—and alas! my only—vision of the work of Gordon Craig. By some chance I had heard, some three or four years earlier, of a publication which he edited, produced and illustrated most delightfully with his own woodcuts. It was called *The Page* and I promptly became a subscriber. Through this I learnt of an organization calling itself the Purcell Operatic Society, formed to revive the works of Purcell, Arne, Handel, Gluck, Scarlatti and others. This Society had already made a start in 1900 with Purcell's *Dido and Aeneas* at the Hampstead Conservatoire. Gordon Craig and his musical co-director Martin Shaw, the composer, were the moving spirits. The illustrated programme designed by Gordon Craig of which I secured a copy bears a note saying that "in designing the scenery and costumes of *Dido and Aeneas*, the Stage Director has taken particular care to be entirely incorrect in all matters of detail." Such was the gay spirit in which the enterprise was conducted. Next year the performance was repeated at the Coronet Theatre at Notting Hill Gate (one of those convenient theatres a little away from the centre of the town which was then regularly visited by all the best touring companies—it has long since succumbed to the cinema[18]) and to it was added Purcell's *Masque of Love* from the opera *Dioclesian*. With the third venture came my chance. At the Great Queen Street Theatre in March 1902 the Society produced Handel's *Acis and Galatea* together with the *Masque of Love*.

So great was the impression which Craig's staging made on me that I find it hard to believe I should not be equally impressed were I to meet it today, after years in which so many experiments have been made in the unrealistic staging of plays. At the time, of course, it had an absolute novelty. Irving and Tree with their lavish expenditure had always aimed at a more and more intense realism, and all other theatres had followed this example so far as their means allowed. Craig's plain backcloth carried right up to the flies, with adroitly used lighting which was yet never obtrusive, his fantastic costumes and carefully arranged movements and gesture transported one immediately into a mood of fantasy, into a world in which anything might happen. I remember especially the enormous cowled giant Polyphemus, singing the famous air "O ruddier than the Cherry" in the second act of *Acis and Galatea*, and the surprising invention which, when the curtain was drawn up on *The Masque of Love*, had placed a huge barred window across the entire front of the stage. As the action of the masque proceeded this window was raised. I felt I could have watched the performance again and again, and wondered that the theatre was not crowded at every performance. I am puzzled to this day, to understand why there was not sufficient support from the public even to keep the theatre open for the fortnight's run which had, apparently, been expected. The production was enthusiastically praised by Arthur Symons in the *Academy*,[19] and by Max Beerbohm in the *Saturday Review*,[20] but these praises in weekly journals came too late; the performances had ended with the first week. How the daily press had received them I do not know, as in those days I rarely opened a newspaper. I still possess the Souvenir, which I think I bought in the theatre. This—a marvellous shilling's worth—contains many of Craig's drawings for costume designs, some of them in colour. For the scenes and the action one has to be contented with Arthur Symons's vivid description in the *Monthly Review* of the following June, which he afterwards expanded and reprinted in *Studies in Seven Arts*, and with Graham Robertson's tribute in the first edition of Gordon Craig's pamphlet on *The Art of the Theatre*.

So within three months I had had my first experience of the two influences which, in their different manners, were to revolutionize the theatre of my time: the realistic drama of Bernard Shaw and Granville Barker, the unrealistic stage-craft of Gordon Craig. The first, as will be seen, spread directly from the tentative experiments of the Stage Society; the second, rejected at first by the London theatre, found a welcome in the European continent, whence its influence—though in a diluted form—reached England some ten years later. And for a time I had little more. My father had fancied that a business career might suit me and for about a year I had been working in the London office of an Indian bank. Whether it was that I found the work distasteful or that I was too assiduous in my attendance at theatres, I am not sure, but something had brought on a severe attack of insomnia and a doctor whom I consulted prescribed a country holiday. This meant that I missed the Stage Society's presentation of Maeterlinck's *Monna Vanna* for which Lugné-Poe brought over his company from Paris, headed by Mme. Georgette Leblanc. Once more the Lord Chamberlain proved unaccommodating. No theatre being available, the performance was given in the Victoria Hall, Bayswater,[21] a small building which has survived many changes of name and is now known as the Twentieth Century Theatre.[22] This recalcitrance brought forth a letter of protest to the *Times*,[23] which was signed by Swinburne, George Meredith and Thomas Hardy, then the three most highly esteemed figures in English literature, and by a few others including Richard Garnett, Maurice Hewlett, Henry Arthur Jones, Arthur Symons and W. B. Yeats. But the Lord Chamberlain remained loftily indifferent; and opponents of the censorship of plays had yet one more weapon to add to their armoury for use in the struggle that was yet to come.

I must, I think, have returned to London and my bank in the autumn, for I remember being present at the first performance of Barrie's *Admirable Crichton*;[24] also I saw Forbes-Robertson's Othello,[25] and a rather dull play by Mrs. Humphry Ward, founded on her novel *Eleanor*.[26] But it seems to have been a comparatively barren period; the Stage Society was not active until the beginning of 1903 by which time my father had been taken seriously ill with the malady which was so shortly to end his life, and was anxious to have me at home. So for a year or more there was an end to my London life and my adventures in playgoing. I went with my father to various seaside places in search of health, a search that was, unhappily, not rewarded.

Two playwrights have given us their impressions of Granville Barker at about this period. Alfred Sutro, who had perhaps met him in 1900 over the Stage Society production of Maeterlinck's plays one of which[27] he had translated, describes him as "a slender dreamy youth, almost a vegetarian," but with "a bountiful stock of ideas that kept him buoyant," "as charming and delightful a fellow as one could possibly meet."[28] Somerset Maugham, on the other hand, in whose play *A Man of Honour* he played the leading part, was less favourably impressed. In *The Summing Up*, though he allows Barker "charm and gaiety and a coltish grace," he thought him "brimming over with other people's ideas," and felt in him "a fear of life which he sought to cheat by contempt of the common herd."[29]

A Man of Honour was one of the Stage Society productions which I, perforce, missed; it was given in February 1903. I had to content myself with reading the text of the play, published as a supplement to the *Fortnightly Review* for the following month. In April Barker gave, I believe, a most harrowing performance[30] in Heijerman's sea-tragedy *The Good Hope*, and in 1904 he produced Brieux's *The Philanthropists*[31] and—it was the play I regretted more sharply than all I had not seen—W. B. Yeats's *Where There is Nothing*.[32] Yeats had been an idol of mine since my schooldays, when I first discovered his poetry. I bought everything of his I could afford and indeed two volumes—*The Wind Among the Reeds* and the collected volume of *Poems*—went with me wherever I happened to be. (There is a story I was not allowed to forget for some years of my going for a weekend to some friends in the country and discovering at bedtime that though I had packed my volumes of Yeats I had forgotten to bring any pyjamas.) I knew much of his work by heart, and it was bitter to me that I could not see this play performed. Between these last two productions had come that series of six matinées of *Candida* at the Court Theatre[33] which were the fore-runners of the Vedrenne–Barker management. Barker repeated the performance he had given for the Stage Society four years earlier, but the rest of the cast was different. There was, I believe, a guarantee fund for these matinées, but so successful were they that it was not required. Almost immediately after the *Candida* matinées came four of Gilbert Murray's translation of the *Hippolytus* of Euripides, sponsored by the New Century Theatre, an organization which had been founded in 1897 by William Archer, H. W. Massingham and Miss Elizabeth Robins. It had produced Ibsen's *Little Eyolf, John Gabriel Borkman*, Echegaray's *Mariana*, Henley and Stevenson's *Admiral Guinea*, and H. V. Esmond's *Grierson's War*. It must, I think, have been specially resuscitated for these performances. Barker produced the play and gave an astonishing *bravura* performance of the Messenger. By this time I must have been again in London for I certainly witnessed one of the matinées at the Lyric Theatre.

Besides this varied work in the theatre Barker was busily employed with writing. Another play had followed *Ann Leete*; its title was *Agnes Colander*, but it was never performed. I read the manuscript a few years later but remember little about the play except that it dealt with a painter and that the scene of one or more of the acts was laid in his studio.

Granville Barker has himself recorded how William Archer arrived one day at his rooms in the Adelphi demanding his help in drawing up a scheme for an English National Theatre.[34] Together they set to work and produced a large quarto volume which was entitled *Scheme and Estimates for a National Theatre*. Dated 1904, this was produced in paper covers of a tint resembling that used for official "Blue books", and was printed for private circulation only. ("On no account to be communicated to, or criticised or mentioned in, the Public Press.") Only the compilers' initials appear, at the end of a short preliminary note. This book was a remarkable achievement; Barker modestly says that Archer's contribution much outweighed his, but the influence of the practical and experienced man of the theatre is evident throughout. One of its most amusing features is the inclusion of a specimen year's programme of plays—including some imaginary unwritten ones—of which the suggested casts were given, the men's names being taken from parts of London—Mr. Ludgate, Mr. Holborn, Mr. Tower Hill and so on, while the women's represented English halls and castles—Miss Knowle, Miss Tintagel, Miss Hatfield, Miss Haddon Hall, etc. All these had, as it were, living originals; and I wonder if anybody besides myself is in possession of a "key." This collaboration may I suppose be dated roughly 1902–1903,[35] and in the latter year Barker had begun work on his best known—and perhaps his best—play *The Voysey Inheritance*.

Gordon Craig was to make or supervise three more productions in London: Laurence Housman's *Bethlehem*,[36] given in the Great Hall of the University of London, South Kensington, because the Lord Chamberlain's license was not forthcoming, Ibsen's *The Vikings* and Shakespeare's *Much Ado* both at the Imperial Theatre in the Spring of 1903;[37] he also designed three scenes for a play called *For Sword or Song* which his uncle Fred Terry produced at the Shaftesbury Theatre;[38] alas! I saw none of these. Nor has London, I believe, ever again been given an opportunity to see, in the theatre, the work of the artist whose influence on scene design has been enormous.

III

My attempt to become a business man having now come happily and definitely to a close, my desire to become an actor, always latent in me from childhood, asserted itself with some force. Early in 1904 I read somewhere that Gordon Craig was contemplating a School to be known as "The London School of Theatrical Art" and I wrote for particulars. In reply came a charming letter from Craig himself because, he said, I was an old supporter of *The Page*. Instruction was to be given in each branch of the art: "We take the A.B.C. of the thing first and this is not very amusing, but I hope to touch the more interesting part pretty soon." I think I should have tried to join the school, but just at that very time my father died and it became my duty as his eldest son to take charge of the family, and make arrangements for finding a new home, since the Rectory where we lived had, of course, to be vacated. Actually I believe that the School of Theatrical Art did not come into being; Gordon Craig left England for Germany at the end of 1904. Towards the end of that summer I made my first professional appearance in a somewhat lurid melodrama of the type then frequently to be met with in the English provinces. I remember little of it except that there was a scene in which, as a middle-aged reprobate, I was about to make an attempt on the heroine's virtue, only to be felled by her to the ground with a blow from a candlestick. Subsequently I was concealed in her bed—I forget who managed that—where I was stabbed to death by the villainess (my own daughter) who mistook me for the sleeping heroine. Thus disposed of, I removed my wig and mature disguise and appeared as a young man in hunting pink in some later scene of the play.[39] None of this tallied very well with my ideas of dramatic art, but I supposed it to be experience—as, of its kind, it certainly was—and did not even object when, in some Lancashire town where theatre business was not promising to be brisk, a quartet of us, in our hunting attire, drove through the streets and into the surrounding country in a dog-cart. It seemed however a poor substitute for the procession with which travelling circuses always advertised their arrival in a town, and I doubt if it made much difference to our meagre takings. Before the end of the year the tour had come to an end and I had found for myself an engagement with F. R. Benson's North Company. Why it was so called I never discovered, for it visited the south and north of England in about equal proportions and indeed can hardly be said to have shown a preference for either, as the first six weeks or so of the tour were spent in Ireland. The repertoire consisted of eight Shakespeare plays and two old English Comedies—Sheridan and Goldsmith—and all but one of these were rehearsed in a single fortnight before the tour started.[40] It could not of course be considered finished work but I found it very enjoyable, and most of the company very pleasant people, nearly all of them quite young. Our leading lady was American—her name Katherine Boyce; today she is Mrs. George Marshall, wife of the American Secretary of State.[41] With her and her sister who travelled with her for companionship I soon made friends, and when once the plays were in running order we took as many opportunities for seeing the country as the tour offered us. Ireland, Scotland, the Lake District, and then the South Coast—where, at Hastings or Eastbourne, I recall that Katherine and I hired bathchairs drawn by elderly men and tried to bribe them to a race along the sea-front.[42]

In the interval between the finish of my melodrama tour and the beginning of my Benson engagement an event took place in London which I found sufficiently exciting although I had then no idea how intimately it was to concern me later; I mean the beginning of the Vedrenne–Barker performances at the Court Theatre. The story of how these came about has been told too often to need a repetition here. I had not seen any of the *Candida* matinées which had been, in that Spring, the fore-runners; but I hastened eagerly to witness another performance of *Hippolytus* in October, and to the first production of *John Bull's Other Island*, and of Maeterlinck's *Aglavaine and Selysette* in November. Then away I went on tour, missing *Candida* once again and the first run of *Prunella* by Laurence Housman and Granville Barker. All next spring, too, I was out of London with the Benson management, but I somehow managed—for we must be then have reached the English South Coast—to come up for a matinée of *Man and Superman* in May, rushing off to the station as soon as the curtain fell and arriving in time for my own evening performance. This occasion has remained in my memory as one of the half-dozen most entirely satisfying I have ever known inside a theatre. I have seen *Man and Superman* many times since then and have myself taken part in it, but neither time nor experience has obliterated that first impression. From the bomb-shell entrance of Granville Barker, clad in frock-coat and made up with red hair and beard, resembling a youthful Bernard Shaw (though actually the character of John Tanner is said to have been modelled on the Socialist leader H. M. Hyndman), the play drove ahead with a constant crackle of minor explosions which were re-echoed in the laughter of the audience. Barker's ebullience had an admirable foil in the cool imperturbability of Edmund Gwenn as the chauffeur Straker, Lillah McCarthy as Ann, and indeed all that cast seemed to me as good as they could possibly be, and whoever had produced the play—Shaw or Barker—had taken care that it never for one moment degenerated into a one-man show.

Some time in the summer this tour came to an end, and although I had enjoyed the wandering life, I felt I was missing too much by being absent from London. There can have been no productions of any great importance when I returned to London; probably most of the theatres were closed—the Court Theatre certainly was—and all I can remember with any clearness was the performance of Bernard Shaw's "tragedy" *Passion, Poison and Petrifaction; or The Fatal Gazogene*, written for the Actors' Orphanage, and given with an "all star" cast in a booth in Regent's Park on a grilling hot day in July.

It was during this summer, I fancy, that I secured my Reader's Ticket for the British Museum Library; and began to assemble the notes which formed the basis of my bibliography of W. B. Yeats some years later. The newspaper files had not then been removed to Colindale, and I spent very many happy hours in the old cool newspaper room, its windows looking into Montague Street. Not many people worked there, so that one received the papers one asked for within a very few minutes. Besides hunting up Yeats "items", I browsed more or less at random and began to learn something about the resources of that paradise for book-lovers, though many lifetimes would not be long enough to explore a fraction of them. From these delights I was called away into the country, and London saw me no more until the next year.

I must have returned to London in February 1906 for I saw Shaw's *Major Barbara* at the Court during the later part of its six weeks run, which is recorded in the programme as beginning on New Year's Day. And this was followed by four weeks of Granville Barker's *The Voysey Inheritance*, which also I saw, with the author playing the part of Edward Voysey. Read to-day, when our ears are accustomed to the snappy and sapless dialogue of our present drama, the play seems written in careful and at times almost rigid style, but to my ears then it appeared the last word in colloquial realism. Here again, and carried to a much greater intricacy, was that interest in family life and relationships which *The Marrying of Ann Leete* had begun to mark. Marked too, was that faculty for depicting the bold, unscrupulous but completely plausible and morally buoyant man, who appears here as the senior Voysey, and who was to appear again as Constantine Madras of *The Madras House*. With him is contrasted the serious minded, morally earnest, younger man—in each case a son—Edward Voysey here, Philip Madras in the later play. In after years I was to wonder whether Barker was not depicting two sides of his own character—self and anti-self as Yeats would have us call them.

I saw this play as the guest of the management, for, on a hint from somebody, that actors were being engaged for the next Court Theatre production, I had presented myself to Vedrenne, and, hardly able to believe my luck, had been engaged to "walk on" and understudy in something no less exciting than Bernard Shaw's *Captain Brassbound's Conversion*, in which Ellen Terry, for whom the play had been written in 1899, was at last to appear. There were to be, first, a series of six matinées, after which the play would take its place in the evening bill for a definite number of weeks—in this case for twelve. This was in accordance with the scheme under which the Vedrenne-Barker performances were conducted. They had begun, in the autumn of 1904, as sets of matinées only; *Prunella* had been played in the evening at Christmas time with no very great success at first through a natural misunderstanding on the public's part that it was intended for children. A second series of matinées of Shaw's *John Bull's Other Island* early in 1905 had caused so much discussion that King Edward VII had expressed a desire to see it and a special evening performance was accordingly given. Royalty having shown the way, the general public and especially that section of it which patronized the stalls and which used to be known by the generic term "society" discovered that Bernard Shaw's plays were even more amusing to see acted than to read, and so the management was able to revive three or four of them in succession, each for a limited number of weeks. This was as far as they dared go towards the achievement of a repertory theatre, such as that Archer and Barker had advocated in their "Blue book". New productions were always tried out at first in a series of matinées, twice a week; those plays which seemed likely to have a wider appeal would then be ear-marked for production in an evening bill when the time was suitable.

Rehearsals for *Captain Brassbound's Conversion* soon began. The Court Theatre, which had a small and not very convenient stage, as well as other disadvantages, possessed one valuable asset—a spacious and airy rehearsal room, at the very top of the theatre, to which one had to climb many stairs. It was here that the first rehearsals took place, and here that I witnessed the meeting of Ellen Terry and Bernard Shaw of which he has given so vivid an account in his preface to the Terry–Shaw correspondence. Although it was usually Shaw who rehearsed his own plays, my recollection is that much of the production in this particular instance was done by Granville Barker. Possibly the fact that he had played the American naval captain in the Stage Society's performances of the play six years before and so knew exactly what Shaw wanted may have been the reason. It was the first time that I had seen a real producer at work, and it was a revelation. I had read the play and knew it fairly well, and it seemed to me that Barker was getting from each member of the cast just that intonation and that timing in the delivery of the lines which I had imagined in reading the text. Ellen Terry, although she suffered, as I believe she usually did, from a congenital uncertainty of memory, had a charm which, it seemed to me, was irresistible. Here, however, I was mistaken, and it came as something of a shock to find that Fred Kerr (who was not, I thought, very happily cast as Brassbound, though he had delighted me with his performance of the elder Voysey a few weeks earlier) and J. H. Barnes, a very experienced actor who had played much with Irving at the Lyceum, both detested her.[43] Every time her memory failed her and she extemporized words, or just waved her hands saying "You see, don't you?" with an engaging smile, they snarled and muttered under their breaths. However, the play ran its allotted twelve weeks, which included Ellen Terry's Jubilee performance for which a special programme bearing the names of the cast facsimiled in their own handwriting, and a portrait of Miss Terry as Lady Cicely, was provided. On the next evening she appeared in a special performance at Drury Lane, and her understudy played at the Court.

During the summer of 1906 the theatre did not close at all, being kept open with a revival of *You Never Can Tell* which ran through July and August, to be followed in September by another revival of *John Bull's Other Island*. I had stayed on in the theatre, and one day Vedrenne sent for me and asked me, in that rasping voice which a generation of actors have loved to imitate, whether I would care to become Granville Barker's secretary. The Court could only afford one stenographer and I think that Vedrenne's department kept her busy; besides this Barker's correspondence must be dealt with at odd moments, while he was dressing and making up or at intervals during rehearsal. Why I had been selected for this work, I never discovered. I had no particular qualifications and could neither write shorthand nor work a typewriter to any good purpose. Except at rehearsal, where I was one of a crowd, I had never met Barker at all, and certainly the idea of doing anything in a theatre except act there had never crossed my mind. However, I was only too delighted. Once more Fate seemed to be doing it all and putting me where I would like to be without any effort on my part. So in the early autumn I was installed at a roll-top desk in a corner of Barker's dressing-room-cum-office (accommodation at the Court was limited) and initiated, from one day to the next, into the plans and the working of the management.

Luckily, no difficulties arose. I found Barker very easy to work with and I believe that the help I soon found myself able to give him made up for my lack of technical ability. In a very little while I found I could take over the bulk of his correspondence, so that he had his time free to deal with essentials. The most interesting and the most important part of this work were the letters to and from the various Court Theatre authors: Bernard Shaw at the head of them, then St. John Hankin, Laurence Housman, Gilbert Murray, John Galsworthy (his first play *The Silver Box* was to open the autumn series of matinées), John Masefield and others. Barker seemed to have little idea that some of these letters would be of use to theatre historians of the future, and when he had answered them they were consigned to the waste paper basket. Later on, I induced him to buy a filing cabinet and so preserved as many documents as I could; I wonder if these still survive.

I still continued to act or understudy—mostly the latter—in each play. A number of actors were engaged on contract, forming the nucleus of a stock company: Edmund Gwenn, Lewis Casson, Trevor Lowe, Norman Page, Frederick Lloyd and myself; an actor might have an important part in one play and only a few lines in the next; he might be understudying and perhaps appear in a crowd scene; this, of course, approximated to true repertory work and was extremely invigorating. If there were fewer actresses so engaged, it was doubtless because in the majority of plays there were fewer female parts; but Dorothy Minto, Amy Lambourn, Mary Barton and Hazel Thompson were all, I believe, under contract.

It seems to me now, that while I had Barker's work to attend to—and this tended to become more and more varied—and while I was constantly at rehearsal, either on the stage or above in the rehearsal room, my days must have been adequately filled; but in case time should hang heavy on my hands I was given the task of reading the many play manuscripts that began to arrive at the theatre in ever increasing numbers. I worked from ten o'clock in the morning till some time after eleven at night, with brief intervals for meals and sometimes an hour or so free in the later afternoon. But on Saturdays the Court gave no matinées, and often I was able to put in some hours at the British Museum.

Barker was now aged twenty-nine and though I was actually only four years younger, his experience in the theatre was so infinitely greater than mine that I regarded him as very much my senior. I liked him—it was difficult to avoid liking him—but though I came to know him and the circumstances of his life fairly intimately, I think there was always a certain shyness between us, shyness which was constitutional on my side, and may have been on his also. He was, at that period, possibly through his close association with Bernard Shaw, an active member of the Fabian Society.[44] To me all politics were anathema; I regarded them as a subtle poison which sooner or later destroyed people's happiness and which would probably end in destroying the world. I have not forgotten my horror when once Barker asked me if I would devote a Saturday afternoon to the job of canvassing for some County Council election which was taking place; fortunately I was able to invent some good excuse for refusing. I ask myself now why I was so happy to work for an organization which, although, as a general thing it did not produce plays which were definitely propagandist, had, nevertheless, a tendency towards social criticism, I see that I could fairly easily ignore the matter because of my admiration for the manner. The Court Theatre had at the time reached the zenith of its popularity. Sufficient numbers of the general public were attending the nightly performances of Shaw's plays to keep the theatre at any rate on an even keel, and there was always much excitement and a full house for each new production given in the series of matinées. But if a new play failed to please, there was still not enough support to ensure that the outlay on production would be covered, and it was the Shaw plays which may be said to have carried the rest on their backs. John Galsworthy was the new discovery in the autumn of 1906, and *The Silver Box* was sufficiently well received to be given a short evening run in the following year. The author would sometimes turn up to rehearsal on horse-back looking more like a Devonshire squire than a man of letters. Although he seemed reserved at first, and was a little austere in appearance, I soon learnt to like him very much, more, indeed, than I really liked his plays, which seemed for all the passionate sincerity underlying them, a little too carefully constructed and written. *The Silver Box* is as meticulously put together as a piece of clockwork; not a word is wasted, hardly one has not its subtly placed echo elsewhere in the whole scheme. And it was admirably acted and most effective in performance. What was it that led me to say to myself, as I can remember saying one afternoon soon after, "It was perfectly done—but was it *really* worth doing?" That, however, was a private question and I am not sure I have ever found the answer. Anyhow, *The Silver Box* was a very remarkable first play. Galsworthy told me that he had been induced to write it by a feeling of impatience after seeing the performance of one of Pinero's plays, which had seemed to him a mere artifice, lacking in any real humanity. He had made one previous attempt at writing a play but had, so he told me, left it unfinished.

Until the next play came on, *The Charity that Began at Home*, I don't think I had ever met its author, St. John Hankin, though I felt I knew him through the voluminous letters in a thin spidery writing that had been coming to the theatre on the subject of the play's casting. It would not have been easy to find two men more unlike than Galsworthy and Hankin, yet each in his way was a typical English product. Hankin was tall, thin, and spoke in a casual kind of drawl; it was, I think, his foible to take a rather cynical view of the world. His eyelids drooped, his complexion was oddly yellow and he wore a thin drooping moustache. These characteristics gave him a peculiarly Chinese look. I used to say in joke—though not to him—that his name was doubtless properly to be spelt Han-Kin. He had written parodies for *Punch* which had been republished in volume form;[45] his first produced play, *The Two Mr. Wetherbys*, had been given by the Stage Society in 1903, and had achieved much success on tour in Australia and New Zealand; I believe it was played in America also, but it seems not to have been revived in England. He had been a member of the Stage Society's Managing Committee since 1903 and for a time I believe he edited the *Stage Society News*, a little periodical circulated among the Society's members. His second play *The Return of the Prodigal* had been successfully given for matinées at the Court in 1905 with A. E. Matthews as the Prodigal and Dennis Eadie as the disagreeable but 'good' brother who had stayed at home. Hankin had a gift for writing easy, natural, witty dialogue and could suggest character with a few deft strokes: his plays have something of the quality of a good dry sherry. Looking at them again recently (for they were published after his death in three handsome volumes with a somewhat hesitating and apologetic introduction by John Drinkwater) I have been surprised to find how fresh they are, how little dated, after the lapse of forty years or so. *The Charity that Began at Home* which immediately followed *The Silver Box* that autumn of 1906 was more to my taste than its predecessor. This presented another of those situations which were Hankin's special field, 'respectable' people in a predicament. It pointed no particular moral, except perhaps that one should beware of one's good impulses, and I suppose that was why I liked it. The Court Theatre public, however, didn't share my liking, and the play disappeared after its eight performances were done.

Talking with Hankin one day—probably during the period of rehearsal—I asked him whether he had read Galsworthy's lately published novel *The Man of Property*. Yes, Hankin said, he had—and added gently, "I suppose the Forsytes must represent his own family—he hates them so." Both the comment and the manner of the delivery were typical Hankin.

In the following year his *Return of the Prodigal* was given an evening run at the Court but audiences failed to support its revival and the four weeks announced were curtailed to less than two, much to the author's chagrin. I am not sure if his next plays were refused by the Court theatre management; they were both produced by the Stage Society, in 1907 and 1908,[46] and not long afterwards we were all deeply shocked to hear that he had committed suicide by drowning, for reasons which still remain obscure.[47] Granville Barker was especially grieved, and when his first volume of plays was published in 1909 it bore the dedication, "to the memory of my fellow-worker, St. John Hankin."

Hitherto all the Shaw plays put on at the Court since I had worked there had been revivals. But now came the rehearsals for his newest and latest piece *The Doctor's Dilemma*. Shaw himself, "that spring-heeled marcher," (Sir Max Beerbohm's acute phrase unerringly depicts him as he was then) arrived with the typescript and read us the play in the Court rehearsal room. A reading by him was almost a performance in itself; the play, it may be recalled, is very long, yet at the finish he appeared to be as fresh and alert as when he started. The cast had been very carefully selected; it would have been difficult to find better representatives of the six different doctors. Eric Lewis, who played Bloomfield Bonington, scandalized everybody by appearing word-perfect at the second rehearsal. In the part of Dubedat Granville Barker was at his very best; I have never known anybody so capable of combining impudence and charm, and his death scene was harrowing. It may be remembered that the scene of the epilogue in this play is laid in a picture gallery where a show of Dubedat's work is being held. A week or ten days before production Barker asked me to arrange this; it is, I think, typical of the sort of thing he was beginning to expect from me. Fortunately I bethought me of the Carfax Gallery which I had visited several times, especially for its exhibitions of Max Beerbohm's caricatures and the drawings of Aubrey Beardsley's. I called there and soon managed to interest Robert Ross, who was one of the directors of the gallery, in what I wanted. He gave me invaluable help, lent us screens and produced from portfolios and other hiding places a sufficient number of paintings, drawings and sketches, to make a realistic and representative exhibition. It is however not, perhaps, surprising that Max Beerbohm (who may have been in the know!) should observe in his notice of the play that "Dubedat seems to have caught, in his brief lifetime, the various styles of *all* the young lions of the Carfax Gallery."[48]

The Doctor's Dilemma was very successful, and began the new year with a six weeks' run; but it seemed as though the climax had now been reached, for the new productions that followed were (with one exception) not very much to the taste of the enthusiastic yet strangely fickle public which had learnt its way to Sloane Square. A new dramatist had been found in John Masefield whose first play in three short scenes *The Campden Wonder* was staged as an afterpiece to a very light comedy (it was so described on the programme) called *The Reformer*.[49] This might have done well, in spite of its tenuity, but the grim horror of Masefield's powerful play struck the audience dumb, and the curtain fell in dead silence—the only time in my life I can remember this to have happened. Yet the play had been magnificently acted; the grim malignity of Norman McKinnel as the elder brother and the heartrending pathos of H. R. Hignett as the younger haunted me for many days. Nor was a production of Shaw's early play *The Philanderer* much more successful; possibly it seemed to the Court audience rather thin fare after *Man and Superman*, *Major Barbara* and the very recent *Doctor's Dilemma*.

It came back again, however, that audience for the matinées of *Hedda Gabler* which followed in March, Mrs. Patrick Campbell at her very best as Hedda; a performance almost if not quite equalled by Laurence Irving in the part of Eilert Lövborg. Now Granville Barker had been a member of Mrs. Campbell's company some years earlier when she toured a play by Constance Fletcher, *The Canary*, and had brought an action against her for some arrears of salary, if I rightly remember.[50] Whether this memory may still have rankled I am not sure, but whatever the cause, during rehearsals Mrs. Campbell was at her most fiendish; poor James Hearn, a brilliant character actor who played much at the Court, had in especial, a very bad time with her.[51] Nevertheless her performance was brilliant. The personal dislike I acquired for her during this period vanished entirely a couple of years later when I met her again in different conditions and learnt to know her better.[52]

Elizabeth Robins, who had made a great name for herself as an actress of Ibsen in the early nineties of the last century, had long left the stage to devote herself to novel-writing. I remember what I believe to have been her last stage appearance (and that after some years of retirement), as the blind nurse in Stephen Phillips's *Paolo and Francesca* at the St. James's Theatre in 1902.[53] Now she came forward as a playwright with "a dramatic tract" called *Votes for Women!* and this followed Ibsen's play in the matinée series. The scene of the second act was a meeting in Trafalgar Square at which a series of orators speechified from the plinth of Nelson's Column. Barker had taken immense pains with this; each member of the crowd that faced and from time to time interrupted and heckled the speakers was provided with a separate individuality and with interpolated lines to speak, yet the whole had a spontaneity and naturalness far removed from the usual drilled effect that is apt to attend crowd scenes on the stage. So successful were the matinées that for once the rigid rule of adherence to a time table was broken, and the play was put at once into the evening bill in place of St. John Hankin's *Return of the Prodigal*.

In the audience one day was the late Otto Kahn who was at that time taking an active part in preparing plans for a "millionaire's theatre", to be run on repertory lines, for New York. He at once desired to make the acquaintance of the man responsible for that crowd scene, and this, in turn, led to Barker's being offered the position of managing director of the theatre. Some time—I think it was in the following year[54]—he visited New York to discuss this offer, but decided that the theatre was far too large for the purpose it was intended to serve. It must have been a tempting offer, for the emoluments of such an affair would have been large and by that time the Vedrenne–Barker organization was by no means in a flourishing financial condition; but I believe he was justified in the event, for the theatre had soon to be devoted to other, more spectacular, purposes.

In the spring of 1907, meanwhile, Barker's new play *Waste* was on the stocks and he was anxious to be at work on it, hoping to finish it in time for production that autumn. It so happened that Robert Loraine, who had been successfully playing *Man and Superman* in America since 1905, now returned to England, and, I think at Shaw's suggestion, it was arranged that he should play Tanner in yet another revival of the play, thus setting Barker free to retire to the country and his writing.[55] From Fernhurst in Surrey, where he had taken a small furnished house from the first Mrs. Bertrand Russell, a sister of Logan Pearsall Smith, I used to receive such requests as, "What I want is a red ordnance map of this district. And I want Belloc's *Path to Rome*." Or "Has Gore or any sensible person written anything on disestablishment (in favour) from the Church point of view?"[56] Another said "More trouble. I have bought a dog... it will arrive at Marylebone Station on Wednesday at 11.52. Will you send a trusty messenger to meet it, have it brought to the Court, be kind to it for the afternoon—without encouraging it to like the theatre as a profession—and have it despatched by the 5.0 o'clock to Haslemere." And a typical one: "On the shelves at the back of my bed is an envelope in Shaw's hand; in it a circular signed by twenty millionaires. Wire me the

name that is marked. I have forgotten it as usual. I am writing to the Porter to let you in."
I find I have scribbled Otto H. Kahn on the envelope of this; evidently pourparlers about
the American theatre project were beginning.

Bernard Shaw has somewhere put it on record that he preferred Loraine's performance
in *Man and Superman* in the first half of the play and Granville Barker's in the second.[57]
Personally I did not like Loraine's John Tanner. He had already played the part many
hundred times in America and had made it a 'star part'. But his method—which seemed
to me to consist in charging at the part, head down, as if he were taking part in a rough
football game—did not fit easily into the delicate framework of production which, under
Barker's hands, had made the Court the Mecca for playgoers who cared about good
acting and a balanced interpretation of a play. He disregarded, too, Shaw's stage
direction which called for red hair and beard, and appeared clean shaven, looking, at that
time, rather like an ingenuous school boy.[58] Where Barker had been wittily impudent, he
was, it seemed to me, just boorishly rude. I was saddened.

Close on the heels of this revival came the presentation of the "Hell Scene" which
forms most of the long third act of *Man and Superman*, and which had hitherto been
omitted; the play being so constructed that this act can be left out without damage. In this
Loraine made a fine figure of Don Juan, and achieved an astonishing feat of memoriza-
tion. He found it necessary, I remember, to go through the part at his hotel with the
assistant stage manager, on each morning before the matinée at which the play was given.
It seems to me possible that it was just because he was playing here a long and difficult
part with which he was unfamiliar, that I liked him as Don Juan very much better than I
had liked him as John Tanner. Charles Ricketts designed costumes of a rich loveliness
which were shown to perfection against a black velvet backcloth.

These performances, given with Shaw's *Man of Destiny*, brought the Vedrenne–Barker
occupation of the Court to an end.[59] Arrangements had been made to move to the Savoy
Theatre in the autumn.

About a week after the closing of the season a Complimentary Dinner to Vedrenne and
Barker was given at the Criterion Restaurant, with the Earl of Lytton in the chair. This
function I am sorry to remember I missed, for after eighteen months hard work, both day
and night, and with the prospect of more of the same sort in the autumn, I had hurried
away to Cornwall and the sea as soon as I was free. An elaborate souvenir of the dinner
was printed, complete with portraits of the two honoured guests, seating plan of the
tables and verbatim reports of all the speeches. It is curious to note that among many
representatives of literature, art and drama who attended, there were only two
actor-managers. Beerbohm Tree, however, who was one of them and who had always
shown himself sympathetic to the newer drama—he had produced both Ibsen and
Maeterlinck in earlier days—made a brilliantly amusing speech in proposing the health of
the Court Theatre authors, and Bernard Shaw's reply, in his best fighting style, pointed
out how little encouragement the Vedrenne–Barker enterprise had received from the
Press.[60]

Before the season at the Court had finished a young publisher, Frank Sidgwick, who
had been for some time partner with A. H. Bullen, the Elizabethan scholar, at the
Shakespeare Head Press, and who now looked after the London end of the business
wrote to Barker to say he wanted to publish a book on the Court achievements and had
commissioned Desmond MacCarthy to write it. I had already made Sidgwick's acquaintance, for he had published *Prunella* by Laurence Housman and Barker at the end of 1906
and was one of the Court's most enthusiastic supporters. Tall and gentle, he had a look of
his uncle Arthur Balfour, and was full of fun and learning, his father being Henry
Sidgwick the Cambridge Professor of Moral Philosophy and his mother the Principal of
Newnham. We made friends easily, sharing a taste for books and an admiration for W. B.
Yeats, whose books Bullen now published. Sidgwick at that time had an office facing the
British Museum, and when I could spare time to go so far I used to meet him for lunch at
the Vienna Café, which then stood at the peninsular point in Holborn, opposite Mudie's

Library. The café has long since disappeared, the site being taken by a bank; I believe it suffered further damage in the second World War. Thither would come also R. B. McKerrow, the bibliographer and authority on Elizabethan literature, and others who might be working in the Museum library. From Sidgwick I first heard of A. H. Bullen's plan for a Yeats collected edition, news which pleased and excited me.

Desmond MacCarthy soon turned up at the Court Theatre; I find a note from Barker asking me to tell him anything he wanted to know, and I suppose I did so. He was then, I fancy, writing for the *Speaker*, but was only beginning that career which was to prove him one of the acutest and most accomplished literary and dramatic critics of our time. His book on the Court duly appeared that year 1907; it is full of good criticism of much more than topical interest, and deserves to be reissued.[61] I had some small share in it since it fell to my lot to compile the programmes reprinted at the end of the book, a job over which I took immense trouble. Thanks to Sidgwick's enterprise in projecting the book and securing the right man to write it, the work done at the Court Theatre by Granville Barker can never be forgotten. Most of the plays given there have been printed, and with the aid of Desmond MacCarthy's commentary and criticism it is still possible to visualize them in performance.

No such record was made of the Savoy season and the few performances given elsewhere.

IV

For some time both partners had been anxious to move the Vedrenne–Barker performances to a larger theatre. Although each had drawn an agreed weekly sum from the Court enterprise, which in Barker's case was increased when he acted, yet the rewards of so much hard work were meagre and it was hoped that by attracting larger audiences a more adequate return might be secured. Also Barker was more and more anxious to withdraw from acting and to have more free time to devote to his writing.

But although it seemed that the goodwill of the public was assured, and although there seems no reason why a move to a slightly larger,[62] a better equipped and a more central theatre should have had anything but a beneficial effect, it seemed that something was lost—that impalpable thing, the "atmosphere", had been changed.

It would, perhaps, have been wise to open the new season with a new play; but for the regular evening performances yet another revival of *You Never Can Tell* was staged, while the matinée series began with John Galsworthy's second play *Joy*. Vedrenne's eyes had been giving him trouble and before we left the Court he used to ask me, from time to time, to go to his flat and read aloud to him plays under consideration. Thus I had read both *Joy* and *Strife*, another new product from Galsworthy's pen. "You read too well," Vedrenne used to say. "You can make a bad play sound like a good one!" Be that as it may, Vedrenne's judgement of plays was here in fault, for though he considered *Strife* a fine play (as, indeed, of its kind, it is) he thought that *Joy* was a more likely money-maker. Had he reversed his opinion and had the new season boldly opened proceedings with *Strife*, it is possible that success would have followed. Barker had written to me during the holiday: "If present arrangements hold you are to be tried in *Joy*—if I don't like you, by Jove I shall chuck you far out." The play, however, was a failure and only survived for its eight matinées. After the first performance Dorothy Minto, with whom I had had to play a boy and girl love scene, fell ill and had to leave the cast.[63] Since Barker had rehearsed that scene until I was exhausted and desperate and Dolly Minto reduced to tears, it was a little sad to me to feel it had all been labour in vain.

After *You Never Can Tell* came a revival (for the play had been given some eight years earlier by Murray Carson, though so far as London was concerned it had only reached the suburb of Kennington) of Shaw's melodrama *The Devil's Disciple*. That fine actor Matheson Lang was engaged for the leading part, Dick Dudgeon, and Granville Barker appeared in the last act as the English General Burgoyne. More attention was now being paid to the actual décor of the plays produced. At the Court considerations of expense had restricted the mounting of plays to what was strictly serviceable; in later years Barker once reminded me how shabby the productions at the Court must have looked. For *The Devil's Disciple* he had asked me to find him a scene designer, and I suggested a very clever architect, Troyte Griffith, a friend of Edward Elgar's, whom I had met at Malvern where he lived. It so happened that Griffith had lately been making a special study of American Colonial architecture, and so was able to give us what we wanted without difficulty or delay. I seem to remember the whole thing being done in about three weeks or a month. For the next production, at matinées, the *Medea* of Euripides in Gilbert Murray's translation, the painter F. Cayley Robinson designed a lovely scene in a pale honey-tint, very restful to the eye. But again the audiences were disappointing. Had we been able to carry out his instructions that the chorus ladies "must be draped in the thinnest of butter muslins and wear nothing else," we might at least have had a *succès de scandale*.

Both partners had now other preoccupations. Vedrenne had taken a lease of the newly opened Queen's Theatre (which was at first to have been named The Curtain) and Barker was in negotiation with America about the offer from the "millionaire's theatre" which was now assuming definite shape. Meanwhile Forbes-Robertson had prepared his long-postponed presentation of Shaw's *Caesar and Cleopatra* and was arranging to take it to America. In order not to break the association of Vedrenne and Barker with the Shavian *oeuvre*, it had been decided that Forbes-Robertson should bring his production to the Savoy for four weeks, while *The Devil's Disciple*, which was doing moderately good business, should migrate to the Queen's.

Neither *Joy* nor the *Medea* having been successful, great hopes were fixed on the third play announced in the matinée series, Granville Barker's *Waste*. But now fell a heavy blow; the play was refused license by the Lord Chamberlain and the management had to announce that the performances could not take place. For Barker the blow must have been severe; not only was the work of two years wasted, and himself stigmatized as a writer, but his and his partner's enterprise received a set-back just at a particularly inconvenient moment. Letters of sympathy poured in; and the Stage Society at once offered to produce the play. The difficulty of securing the use of a theatre for a play which had been refused a license was this time surmounted by a lucky accident. The handsome Imperial Theatre in Westminster had just been sold by Mrs. Langtry, its owner, to the Wesleyans and was about to be demolished; there was therefore no fear that the Lord Chamberlain might retaliate by refusing to license the theatre for the coming year, and a few days had still to elapse before the house-breakers began their work on it. Thus two performances could be given there, on November 24th and 25th, less than a week later than the date announced for the Savoy. One more difficulty arose. Barker had—contrary to his custom—written the leading part in *Waste* with a particular actor, Norman McKinnel in mind, and McKinnel had agreed to play it. But he was under contract to another management, that of Miss Lena Ashwell at the Kingsway Theatre, as was also Dennis Eadie and, I fancy, one other member of the proposed cast for *Waste*. Now, in a sort of panic lest she might be treading on the Lord Chamberlain's toes by lending too many of her company, Miss Ashwell refused McKinnel her permission to play. Time was short and in this emergency there was no alternative but for Barker himself to undertake it.[64] To make matters more difficult, Matheson Lang, who had been playing the leading part in *The Devil's Disciple,* had to leave the cast to fulfil another contract, and it had been arranged that Barker should replace him, his own part of General Burgoyne to be taken up by Luigi Lablache, the original representative of the part in 1899. Thus Barker had not only to produce his own play, himself taking the leading part, but to take over another long part and rehearse another actor as well in *The Devil's Disciple*. It was a hectic business; the Shaw play moved to the Queen's Theatre, and Barker's first performance as Dick Dudgeon fell on Saturday night, the eve of the production of *Waste*. It seems to me now that we never stopped rehearsing, and I remember one chilly evening, when everybody else had gone out to get some dinner before the play began, Barker and I and Aimée de Burgh retreated to the wardrobe near the roof of the Savoy theatre and rehearsed the seduction scene at the end of the first act, while water dripped dismally into a tank.

Somehow or other the play was ready in time. The refusing of a license and the Stage Society's prompt action had naturally created an enormous demand for seats—which could only be obtained by becoming a member of the Society. The secretary, A. E. Drinkwater, father of the poet and playwright,[66] was a firm disciplinarian, quite impervious to blandishment, and it was reported at the time that Henry James and two duchesses had had to be content with seats in the gallery. The play, a serious and deeply-felt piece of work, made a very great impression in performance. If there had been many letters of commiseration at the Censor's action, there were now even more of congratulation and admiration for the play in performance. Barker made a selection of the most interesting of these and I had them bound for him in a volume which should, if it has survived, one day find place in a museum. Shaw wrote, "What you have to do now is to publish the three plays, *Ann Leete*, *The Voysey Inheritance* and *Waste*, with a Preface."[67] Frank Sidgwick, who had now formed his own publishing company in association with a Scotsman named Jackson,[68] was willing enough to publish the plays, but there was to be no preface. And this, by one of the queer legal anomalies then existing, led to an amusing little interlude. Before a play could be published it was necessary, to secure copyright, that it should be "publicly performed." When a play had not already been given in public, the proceeding was to give a reading, in ordinary costume, in some licensed theatre or hall, and in as inconspicuous a manner as possible. A play bill had to be exhibited outside the building, and the performance advertised in two newspapers. Barker said, "I don't see why *I* shouldn't have a little fun out of this!" We proceeded to secure as many authors as possible, to take part in the reading, and together we drew up a burlesque programme, a copy of which I still preserve. The cast included Bernard Shaw, Mrs. Shaw, Laurence Housman and his sister Clemence, H. G. Wells and Mrs. Wells, Gilbert Murray, St. John Hankin, John Galsworthy, Gilbert Cannan, and William Archer. Everybody turned up except Wells who was finishing a book under pressure and sent his apologies.[69] The "audience" (admission one guinea), consisted of yet another playwright, the late Charles McEvoy.[70] The version read had, of course, to be that with the excisions made by the Lord Chamberlain's reader, at that time a man named G. A. Redford. Towards the end of Act III, which presented an informal Cabinet meeting, Shaw, who was reading the part of the Prime Minister, had a line, "Charles ... I wish we could do without Blackborough". But this became "I *wish* we could do without Redford", spoken with extreme fervour. The reading began at 11 o'clock in the morning and when it was over Barker entertained us all to lunch in the Savoy Grill, and Count Kessler, who chanced to be in London just then, joined the party.

Next day a friendly representative of one of the big London newspapers called to see me about the performance. It had been advertised, I told him, and he might have been present. Could he have a copy of the programme? I was sorry, I said, but none was now available. He murmured that he would be glad to give £5 for a copy, but I said there were none for sale. However somebody must have been more accommodating than I and the cast of the play was published on the following day under the headlines "Worth a Guinea a Seat" and "Most Remarkable Cast in London."[71] I rather regretted the loss of £5.

No more matinée productions were made at the Savoy, but there was a revival of *Arms and the Man*, not seen in London since the famous first production at the Avenue Theatre in 1894 when it was advertised by the almost equally famous Aubrey Beardsley poster.

SAVOY THEATRE,

STRAND, W.C.

Lessee   -   -   -   -   -   Mr. J. E. VEDRENNE.

ON TUESDAY, JANUARY 28th, at 11 o'clock,

WASTE

A Tragedy in Four Acts, by GRANVILLE BARKER.

(*As Licensed by the Lord Chamberlain*).

Lady Davenport	Mrs. W. P. REEVES (Of New Zealand)
Walter Kent	Mr. GILBERT CANNAN (Of " The Manchester Guardian ")
Mrs. Farrant	Miss MAGDALEN PONSONBY (By kind permission of LORD ALTHORP)
Miss Trebell	.. Miss CLEMENCE HOUSMAN
Mrs. O'Connell	Miss CHARLOTTE PAYNE-TOWNSHEND (Mrs. SHAW)
Lucy Davenport	Mrs. H. G. WELLS
George Farrant	Mr. ST. JOHN HANKIN (" The Campden Wonder ")
Russell Blackborough	Mr. JOY GALSWORTHY (his First Appearance)
A Footman	Mr. ALLAN WADE (his Original Character)
Henry Trebell	.. Mr. LAURENCE HOUSMAN
Simson	.. Mrs. GRANVILLE BARKER (her First Appearance in this Character)
Gilbert Wedgecroft	Mr. H. G. WELLS (Of the Theatre Royal, Sandgate)
Lord Charles Cantelupe	Professor GILBERT MURRAY, LL.D.
The Earl of Horsham	Mr. BERNARD SHAW (Late of the Theatre Royal, Dublin)
Edmunds	Mr. ARTHUR BOWYER
Justin O'Connell	Mr. WILLIAM ARCHER (his Last Appearance on any Stage)

Neither the Costumes ñor the Scenery have been designed by

Mr. CHARLES RICKETTS.

The programme for the copyright performance of *Waste*, 1908.

Robert Loraine was the ideal Bluntschli, the "chocolate-cream soldier" and Granville Barker, at Shaw's special request, played the part of the romantic Sergius Saranoff, for which it seemed to me he was not specially well fitted.[72] This was produced at the very end of 1907 and was played for six weeks into the new year. After that the Vedrenne–Barker performances at the Savoy ceased.

V

There was now a pause. Vedrenne was busy at the Queen's Theatre, and Barker went to America to inspect the new theatre and discuss the offer made to him. I had a line from him there, saying, characteristically, "This is a 'fast' country, but there are points to it and the people." Meanwhile Bernard Shaw had completed a new play, and Laurence Housman had collaborated with Joseph Moorat, whose music had been so essential a part of *Prunella*, in another fantasy. And there was a new play by John Masefield which Barker liked but which Vedrenne didn't. This was *The Tragedy of Nan* and Vedrenne's objection was based on an allusion in it to "mutton pasty pies" about which it was hinted that the sheep had died naturally. But the management now had no theatre. Frederick Harrison of the Haymarket came to the rescue, and agreed to let his theatre, on sharing terms, for a series of Vedrenne–Barker performances. These began on May 12th with a set of matinées of Shaw's new comedy *Getting Married*. It was finally described on the programme as "a Conversation." There had been, of course, plenty of discussion in *Major Barbara* and in *The Doctor's Dilemma*, but this was the first Shaw play to be discussed from first to last. Although given with two intervals, the audience was "respectfully requested to regard these interruptions as intended for its convenience, and not part of the author's design." Brilliantly amusing as the conversation proved to be and excellently played, Henry Ainley as the Bishop of Chelsea and Fanny Brough as the coal merchant's wife being particularly admirable, London audiences, and perhaps especially the Haymarket audience, accustomed to more conventional comedy, were not enticed to the theatre in very large numbers, and when the play was transferred to the evening bill it was only announced to run for a fortnight, though I fancy it actually lasted a month.

Meanwhile a Sunday play-producing Society calling itself The Pioneers, which was managed by an enthusiastic playwright and amateur actor Herbert Swears,[73] had arranged to give a single Sunday night performance of Masefield's *Tragedy of Nan* at the Royalty Theatre. Possibly Vedrenne's dislike of the play melted away when he saw it in performance;[74] anyhow it took its place in the series of Vedrenne–Barker matinées about a week later and was given four performances. *The Chinese Lantern* by Laurence Housman with Joseph Moorat's music followed, and did not have the success I thought it deserved; it needed Dorothy Minto as the little slave-girl, and the trick by which the "Old Master" came to life out of his picture and in the end returned again was not very well worked. With the last of these matinées and the ending of the run of *Getting Married* the Vedrenne–Barker management also came to an end so far as London was concerned. The firm was in debt; Bernard Shaw has recounted that Barker paid out all he possessed to clear it, and that not being sufficient, Shaw himself paid the balance. There was, however, one further attempt to put things together; it was arranged that Barker should undertake a provincial tour in the autumn, playing Bluntschli in *Arms and the Man* and Tanner in *Man and Superman*.

VI

Frank Sidgwick had told A. H. Bullen of my great interest in Yeats, and he had written to me in the previous year asking for information about some of Yeats's uncollected writings with a view to their possible inclusion in the Collected Edition, of which the prospectus was now printed. I lent him what I had and also the notes I had made for a Yeats bibliography, and in April, 1908, a little before the Haymarket season began, he asked me to let him print my bibliography in the last volume of the edition. I agreed, on condition that I might make it as complete as possible; so that when that season came to an end I had plenty of work to occupy me and was able to spend long days in the British Museum. Bullen had asked me to be his guest at one of the monthly dinners of the Square Club, which then met at Simpson's Restaurant in the Strand. Although he was a much older man than I, we made friends quickly and easily; in June I paid him a flying weekend visit, going by train to Warwick where he met me, and walking from thence to Stratford. It was the first of several visits that I made. The Shakespeare Head Press had been established in an old house in which had formerly lived Julius Shaw, one of the witnesses of Shakespeare's will. Bullen had founded it as the result of a dream which he had one night. He thought he was in Stratford-on-Avon and was told not to miss seeing the fine edition of Shakespeare's works printed in his home town. So strong had been the impression made on him by this dream that he had resolved to make it a reality. The Stratford Town Shakespeare eventually appeared in 10 volumes, the work having been begun on it in July 1904 and finished in January 1907. Bullen himself lived in a modern villa, a few minutes' walk away. He was a handsome man with a mass of white hair and bore a considerable resemblance to Mark Twain, for whom he was sometimes mistaken. There was something about him of those Elizabethan authors whom he loved and of whom his knowledge was so great; he was plain-spoken and somewhat irascible, with strong likes and dislikes, and I fancy that his bluntness, which however was never discourteous, made him enemies. He was the most generous of hosts and an entrancing conversationalist. Caring little for most modern literature, he made an exception of W. B. Yeats for whose work he had a devoted and genuine admiration. Although he had been a publisher—as the firm of Lawrence and Bullen—for a good many years he was, I always felt, much more scholar than business man, and he had not enough capital at his disposal for carrying out the programme he proposed to himself at Stratford, "to print only good literature and to print it well". One difficulty I had to face in the production of my bibliography was that, since his stock of type was severely limited Bullen did not like keeping it set up a moment longer than he need; he was therefore constantly pressing me to let him have final proofs with the least possible delay. In so meticulous a matter as bibliography there are frequently tiny points of detail to be verified at the last moment and to be hurried over proof-reading is a mild form of torture. However the job was done in time somehow and I believe there are very few mistakes in it, though I had to regret some unavoidable omissions. Besides printing the bibliography in the last of the eight Yeats volumes, beautiful in their binding of vellum and grey linen, Bullen produced it in a small separate edition of 60 copies. Although he had edited many of the Elizabethan dramatists and seemed to have their words at his fingers' ends, Bullen belonged to that generation of scholars which paid no attention whatever to the fact that the plays were written for the theatre. He himself, I think, actively disliked seeing plays performed and although he lived at Stratford he hardly ever attended the Memorial Theatre. The only time I heard him at all enthusiastic about anything theatrical was when he spoke of a company playing in a "portable" theatre—a booth—which occasionally visited Stratford. This belonged to a Mrs. Sinclair and was, I believe, more or less a family affair. A couple of years after the Yeats edition was published I had an invitation to come down to see this company. Bullen wrote: "I hope they will put on that terrific piece 'Maria Marten and the Red Barn.' Will Sinclair is really a good actor; I would rather see him than a hundred

1 Pencil sketch of Allan Wade apparently drawn in his thirties.

2 Granville Barker as Frank and Madge McIntosh as Vivie in the Stage Society
production of *Mrs Warren's Profession*, 1902.

3 Sketch of J. E. Vedrenne by the Hon. John Collier, made on the back of an
envelope over a lunch with Tonie Edgar Bruce.

4 Arthur Symons in 1901.

5 Henry Ainley as Malvolio in Barker's *Twelfth Night*, 1912.

6 Lillah McCarthy as Hermione in Barker's *The Winter's Tale*, 1912.

7 The fairy court in Barker's *A Midsummer Night's Dream*, 1914.

8 Wish Wynne as Janet Cannot in *The Great Adventure* by Arnold Bennett, 1913.

Bensons." Unfortunately I couldn't get away from London just then, being immersed in work with Charles Frohman's Repertory season at the Duke of York's Theatre. But to that time I have not yet come.

Bullen was anxious that I should give up theatre work and join him in running the Shakespeare Head Press; but this I hesitated to do. It would have needed more capital than I could have produced; and I was still sufficiently optimistic about the chances of the 'new movement' as it was called, in spite of the Vedrenne–Barker collapse, not to want to make so drastic a change. The Press struggled on under Bullen's management for a number of years; he spent much vain endeavour trying to get it endowed as a Shakespeare memorial; and in the meantime produced a number of valuable books, notably the two volumes of W. J. Lawrence's studies on *The Elizabethan Playhouse*; Yeats's *Plays for an Irish Theatre* with Gordon Craig's illustrations, and a six-volume edition of the works of Mrs. Aphra Behn. In the end the Press was taken over by B. H. Blackwell and moved its headquarters to Oxford.

The August of that year I spent as usual in North Cornwall, and one day received a note from Granville Barker to say he was on a four days' walking tour to Padstow with the Galsworthys. Could I get over to dinner at Tintagel that night, or failing that to breakfast next morning at 7.30? My uncle, who was a doctor, took me over in his car (cars were still rather a novelty in Cornwall then and he was the only man owning one in the district) in time for breakfast. The Galsworthys had their black spaniel Chris with them, the dog who appears in *The Man of Property*; as he was not allowed in the hotel dining room he had been left upstairs and during breakfast piteous howls were heard from above. After listening uncomfortably for a few minutes Galsworthy said, "I can't bear it," rushed from the room, his breakfast unfinished, and sat upstairs with his dog until we were ready to start. I walked with them to set them on their way, and as we passed near Tintagel churchyard I told them the story of an ancestor of mine who had been vicar there in the early 19th century. Falling out with his relations, many of whom lived in the parish, he had insisted, so it was said, that his grave should be as far removed as possible from all the other family tombstones—as indeed it is. I was amused a few months later, to find that Galsworthy had used this incident, with slight adaptation, in his story *A Fisher of Men*, published in the first number of the *English Review*.[75]

When I returned to London Vedrenne told me I might either play Philip Clandon, the boy twin in a tour of *You Never Can Tell* which was being sent out, or go on with my job as Barker's secretary and play in the curtain-raiser which was to precede *Arms and the Man*. I wanted very much to play Philip again, but all the same I thought there would be more interesting work with Barker and made my choice accordingly. It was an additional inducement that the company was to visit Dublin; I hoped I might at least see the Abbey Theatre, even if I could not see any of the plays there. The tour began early in September and for a time all went well. In October I was horrified to hear bad news of Arthur Symons, who had for some time been writing music criticism in the *Saturday Review*. I had been puzzled by his last article on "Music in Venice", which had appeared on October 17, 1908; it seemed to me incoherent. Now came a report that he had lost his mind, been arrested in Italy and was unlikely to live. I was very anxious to discover what truth lay in these reports; the only man I could think of who might possibly know something was John Masefield and to him I wrote. His reply reached me in Dublin.

The two accounts known to me are a. That while in Italy, engaged in the study of the Yeats collected edition, preparatory to reviewing it in the *Athenaeum*, Symons was stricken down with paralysis. He was sent, or taken, home by two men from England, and lodged in a hospital at Crowborough, where his case was reported to be hopeless, and his death predicted within three months. b. That while in Bologna, he lost his reason, assaulted a guardia civil, or whatever it is, was imprisoned, found to be paralysed, and, after much trouble, released, and sent back to England, where he lies at the point of death. The former account, as you may easily see, is the more likely to be true. It is a sad business altogether. He had a delicate genius and a fine standard of workmanship.

Symons's own account of the onset of his madness and his experiences in Italy, written very many years later, shows, if it is to be believed, that the second account Masefield gave me was more in accord with the actual facts. If these were not true they were, at any rate, present in Symons's imagination at the time; in March of the following year, 1909, when he had been removed from Crowborough to an asylum at Clapton in the north of London,[77] the same establishment in which Mary Lamb had been confined, A. H. Bullen went to see him, and wrote to me:

> Later I went to see poor Arthur Symons. He gave me a graphic account of how he had been imprisoned for two days in Italy—"manacled, chained by the hands and legs. Three giants set on me, but I wounded them badly. They hacked my feet to pieces." But at other times he talked quite sanely. I felt inexpressibly grieved.

Symons uses almost identical words in his *Confessions*, twenty years later.

In order to have seclusion for his writing, Granville Barker had decided to stay in lodgings while on tour, rather than go to hotels. During our visit to Manchester, however, he found himself accommodation at Knutsford, the original of Mrs. Gaskell's *Cranford*, a short railway journey away, in some small and quiet private hotel. In Dublin, a fortnight later, he began to feel ill and on coming off the stage one night had to lie on a sofa to recover sufficient strength to finish the play. Next day I called at his rooms at 14 Herbert Place and found him in bed; he thought he was in for a bad attack of influenza. Merrion Square was near at hand, where many Dublin doctors have their consulting rooms, and I soon found one to come round to see him. Before long the trouble declared itself—not influenza but typhoid fever. His habit of drinking milk in preference to anything stronger—he was at that time practically a teetotaller—had, it was thought, caused him to contract the infection at Knutsford. After I had arranged with the doctor to send in a nurse—there seemed no idea then of removing an infectious case to hospital—I hurried down to the Theatre Royal. It was arranged that Frederick Lloyd should take over Barker's parts—he had already played Tanner at the Court on several occasions—while I replaced Lloyd as Hector Malone in *Man and Superman* and the Russian officer in *Arms and the Man*, luckily a tiny part. There was, of course, consternation in London. Vedrenne wrote asking me to stay behind with Barker when the company returned to England; Shaw characteristically telegraphed to me, "What cheer? Bernard Shaw." Barker's own doctor and great friend C. E. Wheeler came over. However the crisis was reached in the course of a week and the long convalescence set in. I stayed on in Dublin for about a fortnight, keeping Barker amused as best I could, sometimes reading to him; luckily I am not easily scared of infection.[78] One Sunday morning the Dublin doctor declared it would be well for the patient to have an occasional glass of good port. Being Sunday the wine merchants were closed, and I felt that even if I waited for the public houses to open, the port wine they would stock would probably not be good enough. Suddenly I thought of George Moore, who lived close by in Upper Ely Place. Perhaps he could supply a good enough vintage. So I made my way round to his house and was shown up into the drawing-room—where, to my surprise, I found W. B. Yeats; I had imagined he and Moore were not, at that time, on good terms. Moore, who always liked to put words into one's mouth, came forward saying, "This is very good of you; you have called to tell me how Granville Barker is getting on." "No," I said, "I have called to ask if you drink port!" For a moment Moore was disconcerted, but presently explained that he only drank claret, but that he had a few bottles of port kept for his friends, and presently I was allowed to depart with a bottle of the best he could muster.

I had already seen something of Yeats during that Dublin visit. Both he and Lady Gregory were then staying at the Nassau Hotel, and I had been there several times as well as to the Abbey Theatre where I had been given tea in the Green Room and a taste of the famous barm brack from Gort. I had seen a performance of Molière's *Fourberies of Scapin*, translated by Lady Gregory into 'Kiltartan' English, and Mrs. Patrick Campbell in Yeats's *Deirdre*; this was during my first week in Dublin, so I suppose there must have been a matinée at the Abbey on some day when our own company did not play one. Later, when Barker was considered out of immediate danger, I was able to go to the Abbey at night and to meet many of the Company. William Archer came out from England. He was a very bad sailor, one of those who does not immediately recover on reaching dry land. The evening after his arrival I took him to the Abbey, but half way through the performance he had to withdraw hurriedly as he said the ground was still rocking. Next day he had recovered and together we paid a call on the late W. J. Lawrence, then the greatest living authority on the theatre. (Eight years later, when I inaugurated the revival of Congreve's plays in London after the manner of their original production he gave me valuable advice about the accompanying music.[79])

The Abbey Theatre company had already visited London on four occasions, a flying visit on a Saturday in 1903, another for a couple days in 1904, and a whole week in 1907—the never to be forgotten occasion when *The Playboy of the Western World* was given at the Great Queen Street Theatre. Now Lady Gregory asked me to arrange for a more extensive visit of two or three weeks, as well as some days at Oxford and Cambridge. In vain I pleaded that I had not the requisite business experience to undertake such arrangements. She would not be put off. "We should like you to do it," she said firmly; "we know we can trust you." So I agreed to do my best.

Barker was now sufficiently on the road to recovery for me to rejoin the company. Bernard Shaw had written me a long and urgent letter asking me not to abandon my post—which I had had no intention of doing so long as there was need for me to remain; but Dr. Wheeler decided that there was no further need for my staying in Dublin. I left it, however, with regret. I had been out to Dundrum several times to see Miss Yeats's Cuala Press—it had recently changed its name from the original Dun Emer[80]—and she had promised to take me to one of A.E.'s evenings. I was no great admirer of his verse, but it seemed a pity to leave Dublin without seeing him.

I was soon in correspondence with Lady Gregory about the Abbey Theatre Company's visit to England. She rarely used a typewriter and her handwriting was extremely difficult to decipher. Though the letters were chiefly on details of business, I had an occasional glimpse of the 'work in progress'. "I am working at a play," she writes from Coole Park in December," and don't know if it will ever come off, and am also translating 'La Locandiera'. My home and Christmas duties claim a great deal of time, and one thinks how good a place gaol would be and that it is no wonder Cervantes and Bunyan came to their flowering time there!" And in a letter of the next year: "Mr. Yeats is working hard at his comedy 'Player Queen' and I am, in spite of warnings, trying my hand at a tragedy, so we have changed places for the moment." I was able to book the dates for Oxford and Cambridge and arranged for a season at the Court Theatre in London immediately after.

VII

Meanwhile a new figure came into the picture; the great American manager, Charles Frohman. It was, I suspect, through J. M. Barrie whose plays he always presented both in London and America, that he had read Galsworthy's *Strife*. He proposed to put this play on for a week at his favourite Duke of York's Theatre, and engaged Granville Barker to produce it. This in turn made more work for me. Frohmann, who never did anything by half, engaged a magnificient cast, the play was one of the kind which Barker's great gifts in production showed to their best advantage and the performance made a deep impression. Unfortunately Frohmann's plans for the Duke of York's were already made and could not be altered; all that could be done was to prolong the run by a week at the Haymarket and another at the Adelphi. Then three important members of the cast, Norman McKinnel, C. M. Hallard and Dennis Eadie, all of whom were under contract to Miss Lena Ashwell, had to return to her management and the run could not be continued.

Just after this I received a letter from the poet Herbert Trench who was planning a repertory theatre for London, asking if I would care to join his company, read plays and take on his secretarial work. Barker had no immediate plans and advised me to accept this offer; but for some reason which I now forget it came to nothing, though Trench's scheme materialized, in a modified form, at the Haymarket Theatre that autumn, beginning with a fine production of *King Lear*, which remains in my memory for the magnificent scenery which Charles Ricketts designed for it. Later on Trench gave a production of Ibsen's *Pretenders*. For some reason or other I saw this in company with William Archer—who had, I think, made the translation—and although the scenery, by that half-forgotten genius S. H. Sime, delighted me, as did also Laurence Irving's performance of Bishop Nicolas, I am ashamed to own that I found the play very long and dull; eventually, I fell asleep under the lea of Archer's tall shoulders. I hoped he didn't know.

Two invitations from the Stage Society to take part in a couple of plays this spring led to my acquaintance with their authors. The first was George Calderon, whose play *The Fountain* was given in March. It was impossible not to like this excitable many-sided man, whose playwriting was only one of many activities. He was one of the earliest translators of Chekhov;[81] he took an active part in strike-breaking during the coal strike of 1912, and was, unhappily among those posted "missing" at the Dardanelles in the first World War. He wrote other plays, and completed the comedy *Thompson*, which St. John Hankin had left unfinished when he died.

The second author was Arnold Bennett, then at the height of his power as a novelist. *What the Public Wants*,[82] a satire on popular journalism, was the second of his full length plays—the first *Cupid and Common Sense* had also been given by the Stage Society a year earlier.[83] One's first impression of A.B. was a little disconcerting. Wearing a high collar and a bowler hat slightly askew, his hands in his pockets, he carried his head cocked with what seemed an aggressive air. But soon one discerned much kindness in the eyes and behind the stammer a certain shyness which the aggressive manner was no doubt intended to conceal. He made few suggestions at rehearsal, as I recollect, and was content to leave his play in the hands of Norman Page who was producing it with the assistance of Charles Hawtrey who had taken an option on the play, and who played in it himself later on, with no great success. With A.B. I remained on friendly terms for many years, and saw much of him during the long run of his *Great Adventure*, in 1913.[84]

I saw much of Yeats during the Abbey's season at the Court which began in early June. He and Lady Gregory came to the theatre on most evenings. At that time the management had been taken in hand by Conal O'Riordan; I find a note from Yeats at this time saying: "I have been enjoying my freedom from the theatre, for now that Connell[85] is in charge I can follow my thoughts where they fancy. I am planning lyrics and all sorts of things—but for that my thanks are to you as much as to Connell. I have been doing little but talk pictures since I came to London—pictures are so much quieter than theatres."

I cannot be certain whether it had been arranged before the season opened that Mrs. Patrick Campbell should join it to play Deirdre; her coming, of course, resulted in larger audiences than might have been looked for, and, contrary to my expectations, her behaviour with the company was as angelic as it had been diabolic during *Hedda Gabler* two years before. She took no salary and was charming to everybody. One evening Yeats went with her to a party after the theatre at some big house, and told me, the next day, how delighted he had been because a man had taken off his dress coat and thrown it on the ground for some girl to dance on. He said, "Wealth exists that simplicity of mind may exist." One day he was lunching with me at the nearby Queen's Restaurant off Sloane Square, and when I asked him if he would prefer to drink red or white wine, he said, "Red—I like to think that Bacchus drank red wine." On this day or another he recited to me his epigram," On those that hated 'The Playboy of the Western World', 1907," and that other addressed to A.E., "who would have me praise certain Bad Poets, Imitators of His and Mine."[86] It was at the Queen's, on another day when I was lunching there with Conal O'Riordan that I met, for the first and only time, Max Beerbohm. During the season at the Court Lady Gregory's book *Seven Short Plays* was published, and she gave me the first copy that reached her, scribbling my name in it during one of the performances. I found her always a little awe-inspiring; her manner was such as I had always imagined Queen Victoria to employ. Yeats treated her with much deference.

I was living at home, my mother having decided, after a brief trial, that she could not bear London, after a half a lifetime spent in the country. So we had settled in what was then still practically the village of Hampton Wick on the river, the place being chosen because it was possible for me to catch a late train home after the theatre. But I thought my mother would enjoy a short holiday in London so took some rooms, during the Irish season, in a quiet Chelsea street off the King's Road. Over the mantelpiece in the dining room hung an oil painting. "Surely," I said to the landlady, "that is a Conder." "Yes," she said; "Mr. Conder used to stay here, and he gave it to me."

When the Irish players returned to Dublin I thought of a holiday, but decided to remain in London for a while because a Royal Commission had been appointed to enquire into the working of the Censorship of Plays, and I thought it would be interesting. The hearings took place in one of the committee rooms at the House of Lords, and I managed to attend most of them. There were a few rows of seats which the general public could occupy, but they were rarely filled. Perhaps the general public didn't know; perhaps it didn't care. In either case it missed what turned out to be a very amusing entertainment. The Committee itself seemed to be about equally divided into those sympathetic to the existing state of affairs, and those who were ready to recommend a change. Mr. Herbert Samuel, as he then was, proved an admirable chairman, holding the scales nicely balanced. Evidence was taken from the officials concerned in the Lord Chamberlain's department, including of course Mr. Redford, the Reader of Plays, from theatre managers including Beerbohm Tree, Bram Stoker, George Alexander, George Edwardes, Oswald Stoll; from dramatists: Bernard Shaw, Granville Barker, A. W. Pinero, Galsworthy, Barrie, W. S. Gilbert, Cecil Raleigh, Laurence Housman, Hall Caine and Israel Zangwill; from critics: W. L. Courtney, William Archer, A. B. Walkley; and from sundry others such as G. K. Chesterton, Frederick Whelen of the Stage Society, and the Bishop of Southwark. The minutes of the evidence as printed in the official Report is one of the most entertaining books in my library.

VIII

Before the end of the Abbey Theatre season I had a message from J. M. Barrie asking me to go and see him at his house in Leinster Place, overlooking Hyde Park. I found him sitting in his study work-room over the old stables at the back of the house; one crossed a court yard and mounted a wooden staircase. At the side of the fireplace, fastened to the wall, were some sort of papyrus leaves which he told me proudly R. L. Stevenson had sent him from Samoa. After a long pause while he reflectively smoked his pipe he asked me if I would like to help in the Repertory Theatre which Charles Frohman intended to start in London the following year; this project had already been announced in the press and somebody was wanted to tackle the enormous flow of manuscript plays which had begun to pour in. "Yes," I said, "I should like to help very much." Very well; I had better see Mr. Boucicault and arrange terms.

Dion Boucicault was equally encouraging. I think he had his doubts about Frohman's wisdom, but he was prepared to cooperate loyally. It was arranged that I should begin as soon as I liked; there seemed no end to the supply of manuscripts. Moreover I could do the work at home, and he didn't suppose I could read more than a dozen plays a week. So that I was able to take my holiday that year with the prospect of at least six months not too arduous work before the Repertory Season began.

Some time in August I must have received a telegram from Lady Gregory asking if I could go to Dublin to take over the rehearsals of Shaw's *Shewing-up of Blanco Posnet*, which had been refused a licence in England by the Lord Chamberlain, and which the Abbey Theatre had determined to perform, in face of stern discouragement from the Lord Lieutenant. I find a letter from her explaining that Sara Allgood had thrown up the rehearsals, and that she had telegraphed to me and at once left Coole Park for Dublin. The difficulty however, proved to be a personal quarrel, Lady Gregory herself took over rehearsals for a time and then Yeats came and took his share. So I missed having a hand in this exciting episode, and indeed had forgotten the whole affair until a chance re-reading of Lady Gregory's letter brought it dimly to mind.

Some time early in 1910 Granville Barker and I were installed in offices nearly opposite the Duke of York's Theatre in St. Martin's Lane. This theatre was to be the scene of Charles Frohman's Repertory, and as Dion Boucicualt already occupied one of the dressing rooms as his office there was certainly no room for us there as well. Frohman had decided to use the Duke of York's in preference to other, more commodious theatres which he controlled because he considered it brought him luck; it was, I believe, the first London theatre of which he had taken a lease. It was in many ways very unsuitable for repertory work. The stage had little room at the sides, all furniture and properties had to be taken below in a lift at the back of the stage, scenery had to be carried up a long passage to the dock doors. With a frequent change of bill this must have added considerably to the expense sheet. Indeed the expense must have been enormous, for Frohman seemed to have engaged every available good actor and actress in London, and many of them drew substantial salaries. He had two producers, Boucicault and Granville Barker, and a number of young artists were to be employed to design scenery. Distinction was given to all the printing used—posters, programmes, letter paper and so on, by Eric Gill who designed special lettering and made a White Rose design. He was then only beginning to turn his attention to sculpture and one day showed me with pride a photograph of a nude figure he had just finished—"I couldn't afford a woman of my own," he said, "so I had to make one!" His brother Macdonald Gill designed the scenery for Galsworthy's *Justice* with which the season opened.

I have not yet forgotten the excitement I felt when Granville Barker began to draft the announcement setting forth the plays to be produced. "*The Sentimentalists*, an unfinished Comedy by George Meredith. There's something to make you lick your lips," he said. Lick my lips I certainly did; and even more when he continued with *The Outcry* by Henry James. Altogether Frohman announced a programme of some two dozen or more plays, some new, some revivals; but I do not suppose he intended to include all these in his first season. He intended obviously, however, to spare no expense, but I did not even then see how on the most optimistic estimate, he could possibly have hoped to cover his expenses.

It is not necessary for me to give any account of the actual productions made, for the history of the venture was admirably recounted in a little book, *The Repertory Theatre* by P. P. Howe, published in 1910. Easy as it is to be wise after the event, I can still feel puzzled at the strange lack of business acumen shown in the way the opening programmes were arranged. Galsworthy's *Justice*, a deeply-felt and very sincerely written propaganda-play, admirably acted and impeccably produced, could not do other than harrow the susceptibilities of its audiences, as it was intended to do. Shaw's *Misalliance* which followed two days later was another example of his 'discussion' manner—he described it as a "Debate in One Sitting"—to which, the experience of *Getting Married* had shown, London audiences were not yet sympathetic. Next came a triple-bill[87]—in itself something audiences were well known to mistrust as not giving them their money's worth; and this was followed by Barker's *Madras House*, another play in which discussion figured largely. It was not until the second inning, as it were, opened with a revival of Pinero's *Trelawney of the "Wells"* that the season began to get under way and the attendances to improve. Another revival, *Prunella*, given together with Barrie's *Twelve Pound Look* (all that survived out of the triple-bill) was another popular programme. The earlier productions were dropped quietly from the repertory. Then Frohmann, perhaps feeling that he must follow up the obvious preference for light comedy, insisted on the production of *Helena's Path*, by Anthony Hope and Cosmo Gordon Lennox, but the play proved too flimsy for even the most frivolous-minded audience and was only given twice. Early in May came the death of King Edward VII; theatres were closed for three days and the Court went into mourning. It was this which really gave the Repertory Season its death blow. One more production, *Chains* by Elizabeth Baker, was made, and *The Outcry* by Henry James (which I had read with avidity) was in preparation; Barker had conferred with James, going down to Rye for that purpose and producing a cut version of the play which poor Henry James ruefully accepted (he alluded in a letter to Dr. Wheeler to the play as "all beautifully and bloodily cut by Barker").[88] Part of the cast was already sketched out: Gerald du Maurier, James's god-son, who was under contract to Frohman was to play Hugh Crimble, Irene Vanbrugh Lady Grace, Charles Bryant, a member of the repertory company, Lord John and it was hoped to secure John Hare for the Earl of Theign. But, as so often before, James was doomed to disappointment; the season came to an end in the middle of June, leaving Frohman with a heavy loss and dealing the "repertory idea" a blow so severe that it did not recover for many years.

While I was still at the Duke of York's, I received an urgent note from W. B. Yeats asking me to take a part in his "heroic farce" *The Green Helmet*.[89] The Abbey Theatre, after its success at the Court in the previous year, had felt sufficiently encouraged to arrange another summer season there, this time of four weeks' duration. Dudley Digges, one of the members of the Fays' original Irish National Theatre Society, and now on holiday from America where he had settled, had been cast for the part of Laegaire, but had decided that he must return to Dublin. There could not be many rehearsals and I was doubtful of my ability to give a satisfactory rendering of an Irish chieftain of the heroic age; but Yeats seemed pleased with me and I think the performances did not fall much below the Abbey standard. It was, in any case, great fun to have played with that talented company, which at that period still retained Arthur Sinclair, J. M. Kerrigan, Fred O'Donovan, Sara Allgood and her sister Maire O'Neill. Mollie O'Neill was then at the height of her power, and it was delightful to see the care with which she passed from Synge's Deirdre, a part he wrote with her in mind, to the aged crone Peggy Mahon in Lady Gregory's *The Image*. And as Pegeen Mike in the *Playboy* she was as enchanting as she had been three years earlier.

IX

My work with the Repertory Theatre had brought me the acquaintance of Dion Boucicault, who had been for a good many years Frohman's producer in chief for England. He was a small neat man with grey hair and a keen incisive manner. There was little about the theatre he did not know and his methods of production, although they were possibly a little academic when compared with Granville Barker's, were thoroughly sound. He was enormously painstaking and gave the utmost attention to detail. To actors he was often severe—never, I think, to actresses—but I found him invariably friendly and helpful. In the autumn he gave me a small part in some adaptation from the French called, I seem to remember, *A Bolt from the Blue*[90] at the Duke of York's. It was not successful, in spite of admirable performances by Irene Vanbrugh and Dennis Eadie (as a French detective.) Also playing a small part in this piece was an American girl then called Theodora Gerard—who a few years later became the rage of London in revues at the Palace Theatre; by which time "Theordora" had given way to the more familiar "Teddie".[91] When the French adaptation came off, Boucicault suggested that I should fill in time by understudying in another Frohman production at the Comedy—I have forgotten its name[92]—and then made me one of the pirates in the perennial *Peter Pan*, which was always given twice daily at the Duke of York's during the Christmas holidays, then ran on for a good many weeks and finally went on tour to the larger English cities. All this was very good fun, though I felt strangely at a loss with so much of the day time at my own disposal.

While I was still busy with *Peter Pan*, Barker produced that very powerful play *The Witch* by Wiers Jenssen. This play, *Anna Peddersdotter* in the original Norwegian, had been discovered by William Archer and translated or adapted by John Masefield. It was given six matinée performances, beginning at the end of January, 1911, once more at the Court Theatre. In those days there was a small seat at one end of the back row of the dress circle which was only sold to the public if the house was absolutely full. It was not very comfortable, and it was usually reserved for Barker's own use, so that he could slip into it easily and quietly during a performance if he wanted to. Some acquaintances of mine had attended one of the matinées of *The Witch*, sitting in the dress-circle. I asked them afterwards how they had enjoyed themselves. "*We* liked it very much," they said, "but there was a man sitting behind us who didn't seem to care for it at all. He kept on groaning and cursing under his breath!" I had no need to enquire what "the man" looked like.[93] *The Witch* was followed, still at matinées only, by a revival of Masefield's *Nan* and, in the same bill, a production of Barker's own one-act farce *Rococo*[94]—once more a study of family affairs and a most amusing one. Meanwhile the author himself was appearing at the Palace Theatre in three successive episodes from his own adaptation of Schnitzler's *Anatol*: "Ask No Questions and You'll Hear No Stories", "A Farewell Supper" and "The Wedding Morning", the first and third of these for one week each, the second for a fortnight. These three, with others added to make a full evening's entertainment were given at the Little Theatre in March, and this opened a new chapter in management. *Anatol* was succeeded by Ibsen's *Master Builder*, but neither of these productions were particularly successful with the public. Once more Bernard Shaw came to the rescue. On April 19th *Fanny's First Play*, described as "an easy play for a little theatre" and bearing no author's name, was presented. Although it seemed to me there could be no doubt as to authorship, there was at first much guessing about it, and a suggestion which found favour was that the play had resulted from a collaboration between Shaw and Barrie. Before this, *Peter Pan* having finished its tour at the end of March, I had been invited by A. E. Drinkwater who was now managing for Barker to "come along and help". Once more I found myself reading plays and understudying; then, after *Fanny* had been given about 50 performances, Reginald Owen who had been playing the part of the critic Gunn (an adumbration of Gilbert Cannan, at that time critic of the *Star*) going out of the cast to take up another engagement, I succeeded to the part. The play was very successful and, although the summer of 1911 was the hottest I ever remember, the theatre was full at every performance. King George V and Queen Mary came to see the play and had to be accommodated in the row of small boxes which then existed at the back of the stalls; I believe that several had to be knocked into one.

Barker now reverted to his system of special matinées; *The Tragedy of Nan* was revived once again in May, and in October a triple bill containing Meredith's *Sentimentalists*, his own *Rococo* and Barrie's *Twelve-Pound Look*—two of these first given in Frohmann's Repertory Season—was given a few performances. When, at the end of the year, the tenancy of the Little Theatre ran out, *Fanny* was moved, without a break in the run, to the Kingsway Theatre where it remained in the bill until the autumn of 1912.

In *Fanny's First Play*, the critics, it may be remembered, make a momentary appearance at the beginning of the play and then are not seen again until the end of the evening, when they appear in a kind of epilogue. Consequently, having arrived at the theatre and put on evening dress ("Don't make up at all," Shaw said, when I asked him) one had nearly all the evening at one's disposal. It was the year when Diaghilev's Ballets Russes first appeared at Covent Garden. The Prologue over at the Little Theatre, I used to hurry off and slip into the gallery, generally seeing the latter part of the first ballet, the whole of the middle one, and a good portion of the last before rushing back in time for my entrance. In this way I managed to see almost the whole repertory. Sometimes I went to another theatre, but this was not so amusing as one saw neither beginning nor end of the play. If I didn't go out, three or four of us assembled in the coolest dressing-room and played poker for modest sums; one evening Nigel Playfair[95] was dealt a royal straight flush, but unluckily for him there was little or no betting against him. He stuck the cards into an album and we all signed it, witnesses to this unique happening in the recollection of any of us.

Early in 1912 came another brush with the censor. A new series of matinées was projected and the first play on the list, Eden Philpotts's rustic tragedy *The Secret Woman*, founded on his novel which had already been published half a dozen years earlier, was refused a licence by the Lord Chamberlain. The play was already cast and in rehearsal; and Barker did not feel inclined to take this rebuff sitting down. He had the support of his fellow-dramatists and a spirited letter of protest appeared in the *Times*,[96] signed by some two dozen leading writers, including J. M. Barrie, Joseph Conrad, Conan Doyle, John Galsworthy, Maurice Hewlett, Henry James, George Moore, John Masefield, A. W. Pinero, Elizabeth Robins, Bernard Shaw, Alfred Sutro, H. G. Wells and Israel Zangwill. This announced that six matinées of the play would be given to which the public would be admitted free of charge.[97] Barker called the cast together on the stage and told us that he would not be able to pay us the salaries for these performances which had been agreed, but asked us to trust him. Of course we all joyfully agreed. The performances were duly given and thus, for once, the Lord Chamberlain was successfully defied. Some years later I believe the play was licensed without question but Barker had of course lost any profits which the matinées might have made. Six months later, when I daresay most of the cast had forgotten the matter—I certainly had—our salaries were discreetly paid us. The matinée series was continued with a production of Euripides' *Iphigenia in Tauris* in Gilbert Murray's version,[98] and then by a delicate and delightful play on a Russian theme, *The Double Game* by Maurice Baring.[99] It was not very successful; but I have often wondered why, when Chekhov plays later met with acclamation, nobody has ever thought of reviving this play, so very much in the Chekhov manner. In June three matinées of *Iphigenia* were given in the open-air Greek Theatre at Bradfield College, and as Godfrey Tearle, who had played Orestes, was not available, Granville Barker himself played that part—it was, I think, the last time he ever acted publicly in England.

Fanny's First Play continued to run to good business all through a second summer, and was succeeded in the evening bill in September 1912 by a revival of Barker's own play *The Voysey Inheritance*, though it still continued to be played for three matinees a week until nearly the end of the year.

X

Meanwhile plans had been made for an entirely separate venture: the production of Shakespeare's plays, not one play only but a series. These were not to be given at the Kingsway; a larger stage and a larger theatre were needed, and arrangement were made to take the Savoy Theatre. A fortnight after *The Voysey Inheritance* had been launched, the curtain was rung up on *The Winter's Tale*,[101] and London had a new topic for conversation and dispute.

Of the young painters whom Barker had encouraged to turn to scene design during the Frohman season, Norman Wilkinson had shown the greatest aptitude and enthusiasm. A tall, quiet, almost dreamy young man, slow and deliberate of speech, he seemed to suffer from shyness to an almost painful degree. We were destined to work together, later on, in many productions, and learnt to know and like each other well, but still Norman never seemed to me to overcome his shyness completely. His father was a wealthy business man of Birmingham, and so Norman was able to gratify his taste for beautiful things. He was, however, no dilettante but a hard worker, and with Barker to encourage him, and a more or less "free hand" in the matter of expense, he was able to give his great talent for scene and costume design full play. Another artist—this time one new to theatre design—was invited to collaborate: Albert Rutherston, younger brother of the painter Will Rothenstein. For *The Winter's Tale*, Wilkinson designed the scenes and Rutherston the costumes. A small apron stage was built out over the orchestra-well at the Savoy, and a semi-permanent set, raised a few steps higher than the apron, with an adroit use of painted curtains, allowed the play to be given in full and without any pause for scene-changes. Only one interval was allowed—this at the appropriate time between acts III and IV, when sixteen years elapse in the play's story. This, in itself, was a staggering novelty for a London audience, while Rutherston's costumes, suggested by designs of Giulio Romano, and magnificent both in colour and fashion, completed their stupefaction. But most remarkable of all was Barker's method of production. He had engaged a fine cast, headed by Henry Ainley, who played Leontes, and had instilled into them so much of his own nervous energy that the play was given with a swiftness of utterance— never allowed to slip into a mere gabble—which in itself made the act of listening a constant excitement and delight.

Even to play Shakespeare without cuts, still more to play him without elaborate scene-changes, seemed to offend the dramatic criticism of the day; unable to accuse the production of dullness, a new stick had to be found with which to belabour such a revolutionary proceeding; Barker was therefore accused of imitating both Professor Reinhardt, whose mime-play *Sumurun* had been a great attraction not long before at the Coliseum,[102] and Diaghilev's Russian ballet. I remember being so indignant at this stupidity that I made a counter attack, which took the form of a long letter to the *Pall Mall Gazette*; but thinking that as I had been connected with so much of Barker's other work my name might suggest that he had himself inspired the letter, I arranged that a cousin of mine should sign it.[103]

I am doubtful if the production, for all its novelty, attracted very large audiences, and the next play to be revived, *Twelfth Night*, went at once into rehearsal. This time Norman Wilkinson was responsible for the costumes as well as the scenes. Many of the same actors appeared in the play—it was Barker's intention to form a more or less permanent company—Henry Ainley brilliant as Malvolio, and Lillah McCarthy who had been the Hermione of *The Winter's Tale* now made a great success as Viola. A special and very attractive engagement was that of Hayden Coffin, who had delighted playgoers for twenty years by his singing in musical comedy but was now a man of fifty or thereabouts, to play Feste. His pathetic figure, as at the end of the play he sang the final song, "When that I was and a little tiny boy," as the other characters disappeared one by one leaving him alone on an empty stage, remains to this day an unfading memory.

Having launched *Twelfth Night* with better success than had attended *The Winter's Tale*, Barker at once turned his attention to the Kingsway where *The Voysey Inheritance* was finishing a run of not quite three months, and there he produced Galsworthy's play *The Eldest Son*, which had been announced as one of the plays to be included in the Frohman Repertory season nearly three years before. It had, indeed, been written in the early months of 1909 and had been waiting its turn ever since. All the author's delicate skill in handling his naturalistic dialogue could not disguise the novelettish plot—the son of a country squire who has seduced his sister's maid and is forbidden to marry her by his father; who has nevertheless just dismissed an underkeeper for the same kind of offence. It ran for little more than a month.

Fanny's First Play which had at last exhausted its immediate public was succeeded at matinées by a revival of another Shaw play, *John Bull's Other Island* immediately after Christmas. It was for this occasion that the author produced his "personal appeal" to the audience at the Kingsway theatre, imploring them to refrain from laughter during the action of the play, and giving a series of cogent reasons for his request. This, in the form of a two-page leaflet, was included with each programme, and has now become a 'Shaw item' much sought for by collectors.[104] Early in the New Year the revival supplanted *The Eldest Son* in the evening bill and ran its allotted three months.

Among the plays which Barker had acquired for production some time before was Arnold Bennett's comedy *The Great Adventure*. It had seemed impossible to cast the chief woman's part satisfactorily and he had paid fine after fine to retain his rights in the play. One day J. M. Barrie and E. V. Lucas had attended a variety performance at the London Pavilion music hall and had been greatly impressed by one of the artists, a young woman named Wish Wynne who appeared in a series of cockney monologues, written by herself. One or other of them told Barker that here was the actress he needed for Bennett's play. Barker visited the Pavilion and was convinced. The next thing was to engage her, and here arose a difficulty, for she had a long series of engagements booked at music-halls all over the country. But eventually an arrangement was made to buy up these contracts, and Henry Ainley being now set free by the end of the *Twelfth Night* run, *The Great Adventure* was launched on its triumphant career on March 25th, 1913. For all the rest of that year and the greater part of the next it filled the Kingsway Theatre to its fullest capacity; it even survived the outbreak of the first World War, and ran until the November of 1914. Barrie and Lucas had made no mistake in thinking that Wish Wynne was the ideal representative of Bennett's Janet Cannot; she was. Even the author, not as a rule given to excessive praise, noted in his journal, "Wish Wynnne a genius."[105] I am not sure that she had ever appeared before in a play, but she gave no indication of being, as she had hitherto been, a solo performer, but fitted exactly into the play's scheme, never throwing it out of balance. Henry Ainley delighted in the character of Ilam Carve. He endowed him with a replica of Bennett's own hesitant stammer, and exploited the eccentricity of the shy artist magnificently. As the long run of the play extended itself he sometimes let the fun of this eccentricity get out of hand—for the part gave him an almost unlimited freedom for exaggeration—which might well have disconcerted a more experienced actress. But Wish Wynne was always as steady as a rock; once her performance was "set", she never varied it, yet it never became merely mechanical but remained fresh and alive—an enormous benefit to the play. When one got to know her, nobody could be more unlike any preconceived idea one may have had of a music-hall artist. If it was a surprise to discover that she lived, not in London but in Kidderminster where, with her husband, she lived a quiet domesticated life, it was even more so to find that she had a taste for philosophy and was enthusiastic about Nietzsche, about whom she would talk to me earnestly in the intervals; I remember her lending me a work by an Italian philosopher, Leo G. Sera, called, I seem to remember, *On the Tracks of Life*.[106] It was anti-feminist, and had evidently been carefully read and marked in pencil. After *The Great Adventure* finished, she returned to her music-hall contracts, and, I think, made no further excursions into "legitimate" drama. She did not live to grow old.[107]

With the Kingsway flourishing, and two different companies playing it in the provinces—Bennett noted at the end of 1913 that his net earnings from plays during the year
amounted to over £8500[108]—Barker was free to turn his attention to his other scheme,
the scheme that he hoped might eventually develop into a real repertory theatre. Bernard
Shaw had written a new play, *Androcles and the Lion*, and with this he opened his
autumn season of 1913. As the Savoy Theatre was not then available Barker came to an
arrangement with George Alexander for the use of the St. James's. *Androcles* was not
long enough for a whole evening's entertainment, so Barker collaborated with Dion
Clayton Calthorp in *Harlequinade*, a charming trifle which has been undeservedly
forgotten. This time Albert Rutherston designed both scenes and costumes for *Androcles*. But although it was magnificiently staged and brilliantly acted—O. P. Heggie, in
particular, giving an unforgettable performance as the gentle humanitarian Androcles—
the play did not attract audiences for more than about two months. It was succeeded, at
the end of October, by a revival of *The Witch*, and a month later Barker made a second
attempt to establish the principle of repertory. To *The Witch*, he added in quick
succession Ibsen's *Wild Duck*, a double programme made up of Molière's *Mariage Forcé*
and Masefield's *Tragedy of Nan*, Shaw's *Doctor's Dilemma*, and another double bill
containing Maeterlinck's *Death of Tintagiles* (which he had produced for the Stage
Society thirteen years before) and Galsworthy's *Silver Box*.[109] For *Tintagiles* Charles
Ricketts designed a very impressive set and equally impressive costumes. The company
adapted itself admirably to the repertory system and the performances ran smoothly even
though, in some cases, there had been less rehearsal than was really adequate. On the
first night of the final production Barker made a speech in defence of the repertory idea
and asking for support to enable him to continue presenting plays under that system. He
suggested that a thousand guarantors of twenty five pounds a year each, for three years,
would be sufficient. A transcript of the speech was printed and enclosed in the
programmes during the following weeks,[110] but the support looked for was not forthcoming.

When the St. James's tenancy came to an end with the year, the repertory of plays
moved to the Savoy and continued there for a further five weeks, while rehearsals were
going on for Barker's third Shakespeare production *A Midsummer Night's Dream*. Once
more Norman Wilkinson designed both scene and costumes, and this time a certain
amount of scandal was created by the celebrated gold fairies. London had hitherto been
accustomed to seeing little girls in gauzy muslins with tinsel wings, and were rather
shocked by these exotic gilded figures vaguely suggesting an Indian ancestry. In his
preface to the acting edition of the play which was on sale at the performances Barker
wrote: "The fairies cannot sound too beautiful. How should they look? One does one's
best. But I realize that when there perhaps is no really right thing to do one is always
tempted to do too much. One yields to the natural fun, of course, of making a thing look
pretty in itself. They must not be too startling. But one wishes people weren't so easily
startled."

These prefaces—for two others had appeared in the acting editions of *The Winter's
Tale* and *Twelfth Night*—though running only to a few pages apiece, doubtless led later
on to the now famous *Prefaces to Shakespeare*. They have a definite value of their own,
and indeed the three little volumes, excellently printed and adorned with illustrations of
costume designs by Rutherston and Wilkinson, were very precious sixpennyworths. I
cherish my copies, and wish I had bought more of them, for now they are unobtainable.
Some day, one hopes, these little prefaces at least will be reprinted.

I cannot remember for how long *A Midsummer Night's Dream* ran at the Savoy. It was
produced on February 6, 1914 and I think it continued to the end of season.

The next Shakespeare play to have been produced was *Macbeth*. For this the scenery
was built though not painted, and I fancy that Wilkinson had made his designs for the
costumes. Had the first World War not intervened we might have seen Henry Ainley's
Macbeth, Lillah McCarthy's Lady Macbeth; as it is we have not even Granville Barker's

preface to console us; perhaps that would have been the play next on his list, for he had intended latterly to devote himself to the great tragedies only.

Preparations now began for a new venture. J. M. Barrie had written a very amusing entertainment, the name of which I have forgotten, which partook equally of play and cinema (those were the days of the silent film), and in which certain prominent politicians such as Asquith and Lloyd George figured, and also such men of letters as Bernard Shaw, G. K. Chesterton and William Archer. Barker was to produce it. A beginning was made with the filming, and some scenes were shot in which Shaw, Chesterton, Lord Howard de Walden and Archer rolled down a hill in barrels. A baby also was to appear (trust Barrie!) and there was a sequence when its perambulator ran away with it. The filming of Asquith and other celebrities presented a more difficult problem. To solve it Barrie decided to give a supper on the Savoy theatre stage to which were invited, among many others, some of those who might eventually figure in his play. Floodlights and cameras were planted outside the theatre entrance, and more were installed in the boxes and at the back of the auditorium of the theatre. A wide flight of steps led down from the stage to the stalls, and after the supper the guests came down these and sat to watch the entertainment. "A Supper In 2 Acts" says the programme. Act I gave the menu; Act II "Frank Tinney's Revue".[111] Frank Tinney, the American comedian was at that time making a great success in London, and he now appeared as compère introducing in his amusing confidential manner, a series of one-act playlets all written by Barrie. "Why? A Conundrum" was played by Marie Löhr and Dion Boucicault; "One Night" by Lillah McCarthy and Henry Ainley; "When the Kye Comes Home" by Jean Aylwin, Edmund Gwenn and Henry Vibart; "Taming a Tiger" by Irene Vanburgh and Godfrey Tearle; "The Bull-dog Breed" by Gerald du Maurier and Granville Barker. Ina Claire gave a single turn. Finally the programme was "to conclude with still another version of *The Adored One* which will be subject to alteration." *The Adored One* was a play of Barrie's which had failed as a full-length piece and had been afterwards reduced by him to one act. But this was eventually intended to form part of the new entertainment; it was played by Marie Tempest, Graham Browne and O. P. Heggie, and at a given moment a rush was made from the stalls by Bernard Shaw, Chesterton, Archer and Lord Howard de Walden, armed with swords which they drew as they dashed on to the stage to rescue Marie Tempest from some predicament. Of course it all appeared pointless enough and Shaw made a little speech beforehand asking the assembled guests not to be disconcerted. The scene was duly filmed, but that was the last to be seen of it. The war and all its consequences put an end to the whole project, and eventually Barrie completely rewrote his material and made it into a musical play, in which Gaby Deslys appeared, entitled *Rosy Rapture*. Only the sequence of the run-away perambulator remained to show that he had once intended to blend film and play into one entertainment.

XI

One day, soon after *Fanny's First Play* had migrated from the Little Theatre to the Kingsway, I was walking down Kingsway and chanced to meet Frederick Whelen, one of the founders of the Stage Society. We chatted for a few moments, and as a result of that casual encounter I was invited, soon afterwards, to take over the Secretaryship of the Stage Society, A. E. Drinkwater, now Granville Barker's general manager, finding that he could no longer spare sufficient time to attend to the Society as well and being about to resign. He had watched over the Society for seven years and under his careful guidance it had prospered exceedingly, its membership being well over the 1000 mark. So that I succeeded to a well-organized post. Attendance at the office could be fitted in with one's other work; the committee met at irregular intervals, usually at about 5.0 p.m, to decide on the four or five productions to be given during the Season, choose a producer and talk over the cast. It was the Secretary's duty to interview applicants for the much coveted honour of acting in the Society's productions, to pacify angry dramatists whose plays had been rejected, and of course to make all the arrangements for theatres, scenery, costumes and whatever emergency might arise. There was an able assistant, trained by Drinkwater, who kept regular office hours. The salary of course was negligible. I had had little to do with the Stage Society since I had played for them in 1909 and had generally been too busy even to see many of the plays they had since done.

[At this point Wade's manuscript comes to an end.]

Appendix

In a note in his original manuscript, Wade indicated that he wanted to include the letter that he wrote, using his cousin's name, in response to newspaper criticisms of Barker's production of *The Winter's Tale*. (See p. 32.) It appeared in the *Pall Mall Gazette* on 26 September 1912.

"THE WINTER'S TALE" AND SOME CRITICS

Sir,—It is a little puzzling to the common playgoer who is not a professional critic to observe the state of bewilderment—not to say irritation—into which some, though not, I am glad to say, all, of our dramatic critics have been thrown by Mr. Granville Barker's production of "The Winter's Tale" at the Savoy Theatre. Surely there is no need for such perplexity. Mr. Barker has simply given us the first adequate Shakespearean production that this generation has seen—that is to say, the first production in which a play of Shakespeare's is given as he wrote it, without cuts, rearrangements, tedious over-elaborated "business," and the rest of it. (I need not complete the list; it would be a long, sad tale.) He has invented or revived methods of staging by which we pass rapidly and easily from one scene to the next; and he has chosen two admirable artists to collaborate with him in giving the play a simple and beautiful setting. What is there so bewildering, so disconcerting, in all this?

The decoration of the play has been called Post-Impressionist; it has also been called an imitation of Professor Reinhardt's work. I could see in Mr. Norman Wilkinson's beautiful and severe designs no resemblance whatever to the pictures exhibited some time ago as Post-Impressionist: the use of primary colours (as in Mr. Rothenstein's costumes) is surely not in itself a sufficient guarantee of Post-Impressionism. Nor, it seems to me, has Professor Reinhardt originated the use of plain curtains and conventional back cloths in stage decoration; I remember, for instance, that Mr. Craig employed the latter with admirable effect in "Acis and Galatea" as long ago as 1902. This is an age of catch-words. One uses such expressions as post-impressionists, Reinhardtian, and so forth, a little loosely in conversation between the acts, perhaps, and nobody is a penny the worse; but should not a critic define his meaning a little more carefully when he writes for cold print?

We have been told also that the rapid delivery of the lines renders much of the play unintelligible. Is this really so? "The Winter's Tale" is not a favourite play of mine, and I cannot claim to know it as intimately as the majority of dramatic critics doubtless do; but I can honestly say that I had no difficulty whatever in hearing or following the lines of the play, except in a few instances, where I believe the fault lay in the performer's actual elocution, and not in the speed. On the other hand, the value of this swiftness to the action of the play was immense.

Why is it, then, that our critics are so perturbed? Can it be (distressing thought!) that Mr. Granville Barker has once more pioneered successfully, and that these gentlemen don't like pioneers? If that be so, why, one wonders, do they attend Mr. Barker's productions at all? Why not, as Mr. W. B. Yeats once suggested, content themselves with those productions which so many clever men have made specially to please them? They have seen Mr. Barker at work for several years, strengthening and revitalising the modern drama and its methods of production; they have been dragged reluctantly to admire him. (Only one critic, I fancy, had the courage recently to reprint his original 1905 "notice" of "The Voysey Inheritance" as though to prove triumphantly that he had not advanced in the interval!) Surely these critics might have guessed that Mr. Barker would be "up to" something when it came to Shakespeare—and stayed away!

Personally, speaking as one who had hoped, almost despairingly, to see a production of Shakespeare that should not cause one intolerable shame, I am very grateful to Mr. Barker. Thanks to him, we may confidently hope that in a few years' time to attempt to present the plays of our great English dramatist in the form in which he wrote them will not necessarily be stigmatised as "German." On the whole, one may say "It moves."—Yours, etc.,

        (Miss) IRENE DALLAS

35, St. George's Mansions,
  Red Lion-square, W.C., Sept. 25

Allan Wade's Later Years

Allan Wade was Secretary of the Incorporated Stage Society from 1911 to 1916. The Society was now well into its second decade, and as he indicates was firmly established. Among the plays that it produced while he was Secretary were George Moore's *Esther Waters* and *Elizabeth Cooper*, Jacques Copeau's version of *The Brothers Karamazov*, in which Wade played the saintly brother, Alexei, Chekhov's *Uncle Vanya*, a double-bill of Schnitzler's *Green Cockatoo* and *Comtesse Mitzi*, and another double-bill of Anatole France's *Au Petit Bonheur* and *The Man Who Married a Dumb Wife*. This latter pair were both translated by Ashley Dukes, and he and Wade shared the directing of them. Granville Barker snapped up *The Man Who Married a Dumb Wife* as a vehicle for his wife, Lillah McCarthy, and a curtain-raiser for *Androcles and the Lion* which he was about to take to New York, where the two plays opened at Wallack's Theatre on 27 January 1915, Robert Edmund Jones designing the France play.

Wade had begun to work as a director in his first season as Secretary when he was responsible for *Los Interesses Creados* (*The Bias of the World*) by Jacinto Benavente, on which he collaborated with Norman Wilkinson as designer. He also directed C. K. Munro's first play, *Wanderers*, the prelude to a long association between the two men, and, at the end of his tenure as Secretary, Congreve's *The Double Dealer*, to which he refers in the memoir.

The Double Dealer was part of a change in policy by the Stage Society. Its original intention had been to produce new plays, both foreign and home-grown, which regular commercial managements refused to risk. But following the outbreak of the Great War in 1914, suitable new scripts were in short supply. Ashley Dukes therefore suggested that the Society look to the neglected comedies of the Restoration period, and this led to the production of plays by Farquhar, Congreve and Vanbrugh. Wade directed *Love for Love* for the Stage Society in 1917.

In 1916 Wade had renewed his association with the plays of W. B. Yeats. A drawing-room production of *At The Hawk's Well*, the first of Yeats's plays for dancers, was organised for a group of friends at the home of Lady Cunard in Cavendish Square. The performance was choreographed by Michio Ito, the Japanese dancer, who had been appearing at the London Coliseum, and Edmund Dulac designed the costumes and masks. Ito had been approached by Ezra Pound, then acting as Yeats's secretary, seeking his help with the completion of Ernest Fenellosa's book on the Noh drama. Following its publication, Ito was asked by Yeats to assist with *At The Hawk's Well*. Ito himself played the Hawk, the Guardian of the Well, Henry Ainley Cuchulain, and Wade the Old Man. Edward Marsh, who was present, described the occasion in a letter to Cathleen Nesbitt in which there is an apparent reference to Wade: "The play began with very atmospheric 'keening' behind the screen and a man in black solemnly pacing to the front—he got there, made an impressive bow to the audience, then started, and said 'Oh we've forgotten to light the lanterns!'—lighted them, retired, paced solemnly forward again, and began his speech."[112] Wade describes the performance, on 2 April 1916, as "in the nature of a *répétition générale*."[113] Then, on 4 April, there was a performance before a larger audience, including Queen Alexandra, at the home of Lord and Lady Islington in aid of a war charity, the Social Institute Union.

During these years, Wade had also been busy in the commercial theatre. He had continued to act as Barker's play-reader at the Kingsway and the Little until 1915, and when *Fanny's First Play* was revived, he had again played Gunn. In the 1917–18 season, he was play-reader for the management of J. E. Vedrenne and Dennis Eadie, and also for Dion Boucicault. He was also business manager at the Royalty for Vedrenne and Eadie.

In 1918–19, he managed Lena Ashwell's company in Paris. There then came an important development.

The War being over, the Stage Society was able to return exclusively to its original purpose as a producer of new work. Wade and Ashley Dukes, together with W. S. Kennedy and Montague Summers, persuaded the Society to sponsor a separate organisation, specifically for the production of older plays like those which the Society had turned to during the War. Thus the aptly named Phoenix Society came into being. Wade directed almost all of its productions, of which there were 26 in all beginning with Webster's *Duchess of Malfi*, with Cathleen Nesbitt as the Duchess, on 23 November 1919. Many accomplished or promising actors appeared in these productions. Ion Swinley often played leading roles including Webster's Ferdinand, Dryden's Antony, Otway's Jaffeir, Jonson's Mosca and Marlowe's Faustus. Balliol Holloway, frequently the baritone to Swinley's tenor as one commentator has it, played opposite him as Pierre in *Venice Preserv'd* and as Volpone, and he also played Subtle in *The Alchemist*, Barabas in *The Jew of Malta* and Horner in *The Country Wife*. Edith Evans appeared several times with the Society, at first in supporting roles but later as Cleopatra to Swinley's Antony in *All for Love*, one of the two Phoenix productions directed by Edith Craig. Sybil Thorndike played the Witch of Edmonton and Evadne in Fletcher's *Maid's Tragedy*. A young John Gielgud appeared as Castalio in Otway's *The Orphan*, Athene Seyler was repeatedly successful in Restoration comedies, Isabel Jeans made a particular hit as Margery Pinchwife, and Ernest Thesiger was praised for the perfection of his performances in parts ranging in their variety from Tattle in *Love for Love* to Marlowe's Mephistophiles. If distinguished acting was abundant, the Phoenix Society had other assets. The permanent setting for the plays was designed by Norman Wilkinson, and the constancy of the physical stage together with the fact that almost all of the productions were made by Wade gave the Phoenix a stylistic continuity that was a rarity among the experimental play-producing societies.

The late Norman Marshall has left us a characteristically acute appreciation of Wade's work for the Phoenix:

> The chief feature of Wade's productions was their simplicity. Nothing was allowed to interfere with continuity of action and swiftness of speech. He reduced furniture and props to a minimum. He seemed at his happiest as a producer with a bare stage which gave him complete freedom to design bold movement and striking pictorial groupings. He never attempted to stunt or fantasticate the plays. He believed in allowing them to stand or fall on their own merits. In one of his letters he refers to the importance of the producer "sternly resisting all efforts to astonish, to scribble, as it were, his own name across the author's page." In the same letter he refers to "my long-held belief that what the good dramatist gives and what the intelligent public most eagerly acclaims in the theatre is, above all and before all, the opportunity for acting." As he had a gift for casting and the ability to teach actors how to speak both verse and prose with rhythm and balance without subduing their performances to recitation, the result was generally very satisfying.[114]

It is easy to recognise in this account a disciple of Granville Barker.

The last Phoenix production was of Wycherley's *The Gentleman Dancing Master* on 3 December 1925. Early in 1926, Wade joined the Canadian actor, Raymond Massey, and George Carr in taking a long lease of the Everyman Theatre in Hampstead. The Everyman had been created out of a drill hall by Norman Macdermott in 1920. Macdermott had retired in 1925 and Malcolm Morley had taken over, but he too had run into difficulties and made way for the triumvirate. George Carr and Raymond Massey were old friends. Carr had been Macdermott's stage-manager and Massey had made his first professional appearance at the Everyman in Eugene O'Neill's *In the Zone* in 1922. Wade, meanwhile, had been busy with the Phoenix Society. He was seen as an asset to the new Everyman management for his sound knowledge of theatre economics.[115]

Massey has defined the triumvirate's policy, or lack of it, as "an attempt to achieve a reasonable degree of quality over an extended period with a continuing number of plays." They had capital of about £3000 to work with, and when half of that was gone they expected to quit. Their hope was that at least some productions could be transferred to the West End. They also proposed to fall back on revivals of Shaw plays when necessary. The only problem with this was that Shaw habitually contracted for a 15 per cent royalty. "But Allan Wade," records Massey, "reminding G.B.S. of the old Barker days when he was glad of the 5, 7½ or 10 per cent which the author normally gets, obtained the only concession Shaw ever made to a professional management—the Everyman Theatre could have Shaw plays at a straight 5 per cent."[116]

Despite this advantage, the Carr–Massey–Wade management lasted for only a year. It encountered two major obstacles, the General Strike of 1926 and the London Public Morality Council. At first, however, all went well. They began with *Mr. Pepys*, a ballad opera by Clifford Bax and Martin Shaw with Frederick Ranalow as the diarist, Isabel Jeans as Nell Gwynn and Margot Sieveking (the future Mrs. Allan Wade) as Mrs. Pepys. Wade directed, putting to good use his experience with Restoration comedy, the notices were good, and the play transferred to the Royalty. This success was followed by two American plays, O'Neill's *Beyond the Horizon* (Wade as Dr. Fawcett) and Hatcher Hughes's *Hell Bent for Heaven*. Wade then set about preparing *Widower's Houses* but before it could open the General Strike supervened. Most theatres, including the Everyman and the Royalty, promptly shut down.

Ten days later the run of *Mr. Pepys* resumed at the Royalty but the break had proved fatal at the box office and its remaining two weeks ran at a loss. The management had now lost half its capital and could afford to lose no more.

For the rest of 1926, it remained on an even keel. *Widowers' Houses* was put back into production under George Carr and was followed by *Arms and the Man* with Robert Loraine as Bluntschli. In October came the *première* of Noel Coward's *The Rat Trap* and in November, Wade directed *The Gift Horse* by J. B. Sterndale Bennett. Then in November came a production of Wycherley's *Country Wife*. Except for the Phoenix production of 1924, this was the play's first production in Britain for 176 years and the first in London since David Garrick's at Drury Lane in 1748. Wade again directed and this time played Dorilant also. Isabel Jeans and Athene Seyler repeated their Phoenix parts as Margery Pinchwife and Lady Squeamish. Notices were favorable and business promising when a lady named Mrs. Hornibrook, the president of the London Public Morality Council, descended on the production. Although the row which followed did not inhibit audiences from attending the Everyman, it did, Massey thinks, discourage managements who contemplated taking the production into the West End. The three managers kept the Everyman going until the end of the season, Wade directing *Jazz Patterns* by Cecil Lewis and *Common People* by Miles Mander, but then each found himself a better offer and the partnership, which was, as Massey says, "barely afloat financially,"[117] disbanded.

Wade continued as the Colonel in Reginald Berkeley's anti-war play, *The White Chateau*, which had been directed by Massey and transferred from the Everyman to the West End, and then he played Asa Trenchard in a dramatic adaptation of Theodore Dreiser's *An American Tragedy* for one of the Sunday night societies, the Venturers. He was in a lengthy run of *Potiphar's Wife* as the Judge, at the end of 1927. In 1930 he toured South Africa with Nicholas Hannen and Athene Seyler, in a repertoire comprising St. John Ervine's *The First Mrs. Fraser*, Monckton Hoffe's *Many Waters*, and *The Middle Watch* by Ian Hay and Stephen King-Hall. Later that year he was in New York in Frank Harvey's *The Last Enemy*. His last roles were Lord Granton in *The Nelson Touch* by Neil Grant at the Embassy in September 1931, and Dr. Whipple in the American comedy, *Cloudy with Showers* by Floyd Dell and Thomas Mitchell at the St. Martin's in April 1932.

But his principal interest in these years was not so much in acting as in directing. Besides his work for the Phoenix and at the Everyman, he directed a number of productions for the Stage Society in the twenties. These included Henry James's *The Reprobate*, four plays by

C. K. Munro—*At Mrs. Beam's, The Rumour, Progress* and *Bluestone Quarry*, Duhamel's *The Mental Athletes*, Beatrice Mayor's *The Pleasure Garden* with settings designed by Duncan Grant, *Raleigh* by D. A. Barker, and Jules Romains's *The Dictator*. He directed Yeats's *The Land of Heart's Desire* at the Kingsway in November 1921, and Strindberg's *Creditors* at the Oxford Playhouse in November, 1925. In January 1928, the Stage Society organised a special benefit to try to raise funds to revive the Phoenix Society and Wade directed Shaw's *The Admirable Bashville* for the occasion. It was also Wade who introduced the Stage Society to Pirandello and suggested that it should produce *Six Characters in Search of an Author*. In 1929, he directed Munro's *Veronica* at the Arts Theatre, and in 1935, his last production, Webster's *The White Devil*, in a further attempt to revive the Phoenix Society. He also translated two plays from the French for the Stage Society; these were Cocteau's *La Machine Infernale*, called *The Machine of the Gods* in English, and Giraudoux's *Intermezzo*.

In two successive years, Wade went to Canada as adjudicator of the Dominion Drama Festival. In 1935, it was to judge the finals of this annual national contest. "Actors, like poets, are born," he is reported as saying, "and judging by what I have seen this week, the birthrate must be high in Canada."[118] The organisers of the Festival were sufficiently pleased with Wade that he was invited back a second time the following year, this time to act as a regional adjudicator and thus he travelled the country. Since Granville Barker had accepted an invitation to judge the finals in 1936, Wade was here restored to something like his former relationship with his old chief. He was among the welcoming party that greeted Barker when he stepped off the train in Ottawa on the evening of 19 April 1936.

In the forties and fifties, Wade turned away from the practical work of the theatre and did more writing and editing. He wrote out his memories of the London theatre in the late 1940s to judge their date from his reference to Katherine Boyce.[119] He contributed a memoir of Edith Craig, Gordon Craig's sister, entitled "A Thread of Memory" to the book *Edy* published in 1949. For Mander and Mitchenson's *Theatrical Companion to Shaw* (1954) he wrote "Shaw and the Stage Society." As a founder-member of the Society for Theatre Research, he collaborated with St. Vincent Troubridge in a series of articles listing early Nineteenth Century plays for early issues of *Theatre Notebook*; he also published there an informative obituary of Montague Summers.

The literary work for which Wade is best known, however, was his editing and collecting of the work of others. As long ago as 1898 or 1899, he had begun making a bibliography of Yeats, which appeared in 1908 as volume eight of the Collected Edition of Yeats, and also in a limited edition of sixty copies, published by Bullen at the Shakespeare Head Press, Stratford-upon-Avon. After Yeats's death, the bibliography was completed and in this form published by Rupert Hart-Davis as the first of The Soho Bibliographies in 1951. Two years later, Wade's splendid edition of Yeats's *Letters* appeared. He made his selection and edited the letters with the interest of the intelligent lover of literature at heart. His own contributions as introductory passages to the various sections and annotations to particular letters enhance the reader's pleasure. It is a mark of Wade's personal modesty that of the letters Allan Wade himself received from Yeats, he printed only four although there are 30 of these in the Lilly Library at Indiana University.

Before the edition of Yeats's Letters, Wade had collected and published Henry James's writings on the theatre under the title, *The Scenic Art: Notes on Acting and the Drama, 1872–1901* (1948). His admiration for James also dated from the 1890s. Having been play-reader for the Frohman repertory theatre, when *The Outcry* was produced in 1909, he recalled that experience for Leon Edel: "I remember very well the manuscript of *The Outcry* and my excitement in reading it, and my conviction that it would be far over the heads of our rather stupid audiences." He added his own critical assessment: "It is true that James's dramatic sense was more in tune with the French than the English theatre of his day—but had he been given more occasion for actual practical work *in* the theatre he would probably have been able to modify his tendency to excessive length and our theatre would have gained a really fine dramatist."[120] In 1919, Wade himself had directed James's play *The Reprobate* for the Stage Society. Death prevented him from reviewing the manuscript of the Edel and Laurence bibliography of James, to which he had also made significant contributions, but there can be no doubting Leon Edel's characterization of him in the preface to that work as "one of the most sensitive of Jamesians."[121] Professor Edel has elsewhere recalled his first meeting with Wade at the British Museum, "where he was found "patiently copying out, in a meticulous hand, and with a refreshing disregard for the photostat (and later microfilm), the novelist's papers on the drama, relishing each phrase as he copied it, living through again the experience of the author himself, rescuing them from old magazines and newspapers in which they had lain buried and unrecognized, some for more than half a century."[122]

Patient copying in the British Museum also brought to light the bulk of Max Beerbohm's dramatic criticism. Beerbohm was dramatic critic for the *Saturday Review* for twelve years, three times as long as the tenure of his predecessor, Bernard Shaw. In 1924, he collected about a third of the articles he had written, acknowledging that in those he had suppressed there was quite as much of his best as in those he had selected. Wade's transcribing of the suppressed material eventually appeared, some years after his death, in *More Theatres* (1969) and *Last Theatres* (1970), both edited and published by Sir Rupert Hart-Davis. These volumes had been preceded by another Beerbohm item, *Max's Nineties, Drawings 1892–1899* (1958), a book which, Sir Rupert remarks in a note, "originated in the mind of the late Allan Wade." This book too resulted from the recovery of material long buried in the periodicals in which it had originally appeared. The original plan was for three or four volumes of Max's caricatures, but these never materialized. Instead, Sir Rupert compiled *A Catalogue of the Caricatures of Max Beerbohm* (1972).

Rooted in the Nineties as his affections and admirations were, it is fitting to think that Wade, at the time of his death, was engaged on another editorial task for his dear friend, Rupert Hart-Davis, which he had begun in 1954 and on which he was working until a few hours before he died. This was the magnificent definitive edition of *The Letters of Oscar Wilde*, completed by Sir Rupert and finally published by him in 1962.

Allan Wade died quite suddenly on 12 July 1955 at the age of 74. Both Rupert Hart-Davis and Leon Edel contributed obituary notices to *The Times*. Sir Rupert described him as "the perfect researcher, meticulous in transcription, indefatigable in pursuit," and "one of the sweetest and most modest of men."[123] Professor Edel noted the unusual combination of the man of the theatre and the bookish man and called Wade "that rare figure, the distinguished scholar, the instinctive man of letters, for whom the delights of literary illumination are an end in themselves."[124]

The key to Wade's character and achievements is perhaps his personal modesty and his keen admiration and sense of responsibility to other imaginations. He preferred directing to acting, editing to authoring. The way in which he worked kept his own contribution subservient to the achievement of others. He told Leon Edel that when he directed *The Reprobate*, "I had only to alter *one* of Henry James's stage directions."[125] It was not only a gesture of admiration for James as a dramatist but a statement of Wade's idea of the role of the director, to resist that temptation to scribble his own name across the author's page.

For this reason, perhaps, the value of his own life and work has passed with less recognition than it deserves. It must be a matter for regret that he left only the fragment of autobiography that we have here, but at the same time a cause for rejoicing that there is at least this much to commemorate a life in the service of the theatre and of literature.

Notes

1 They retired in 1908.
2 In 1900 and 1903.
3 Wade was writing in the late 1940s.
4 Produced by Oscar Asche at His Majesty's on 4 September 1907.
5 See, however, Shaw's letter to William Archer, 7 November 1903, in *Collected Letters, 1898–1910*, ed. Dan. H. Laurence (London, 1972), pp. 361–5.
6 St. John Hankin's review appeared in the *Academy*, 15 July 1899.
7 At the Prince of Wales' Theatre, where it opened, 27 August 1901. Rawdon Crawley was played by Leonard Boyne.
8 First seen in London at the Adelphi, 1 May 1902, with Frank Mills as Jean. The touring production, with Barker as Jean, was at the Borough Theatre, Stratford, London, E., in the week of 24 November.
9 As Erik Bratsberg, Vaudeville Theatre, 25 February 1900.
10 Globe Theatre, 29 April 1900.
11 *Morning Chronicle*, 1 May 1900.
12 As Robert Scholz, Vaudeville Theatre, 10 June 1900.
13 Shaw, "Granville Barker—Some Particulars," in *Drama*, New Series No. 3, Winter 1946, p. 8.
14 Reprinted in *Plays, Acting and Music* (London, 1909) pp. 124–8.
15 Until the revival by the Royal Shakespeare Company at the Aldwych, 18 September 1975.
16 Bernard Shaw presented the manuscript of *Our Visitor to "Work-a-Day"* to the British Museum. In addition to the two plays mentioned by Wade, there was a third on which Barker and Thomas collaborated, *The Family of the Oldroyds*. See C. B. Purdom, *Harley Granville Barker* (London, 1956), pp. 306–7.
17 At Terry's Theatre, 23 March.
18 First as the Coronet; then, after 1950, as the Gaumont, Notting Hill Gate.
19 "Music, Staging and Some Acting," *Academy and Literature*, 22 March 1902.
20 "Mr. Craig's Experiment," *Saturday Review*, 5 April 1902; reprinted in *Around Theatres* (London, 1924) vol. 1, pp. 254–257.
21 On 20 June 1902.
22 "It ceased to be a theatre in 1963, when the fittings were stripped out and it was converted to use as an antique furniture warehouse." F. W. H. Sheppard (ed.) *Survey of London*, vol. xxxvii (London, 1973), p. 249.
23 *Times*, 20 June 1902.
24 Duke of York's, 4 November 1902.
25 At the Lyric from 15 December 1902 to 5 February 1903.
26 Also entitled *Eleanor*, it was given 13 matinée performances at the Royal Court Theatre between 30 October and 15 November 1902.
27 *The Death of Tintagiles*.
28 *Celebrities and Simple Souls* (London, 1933), p. 115.
29 *The Summing Up* (London, 1948) p. 112. Barker played Basil Kent.
30 As Barend. "Many moving and intensely painful moments are likely to remain in the memory of people who had the advantage of seeing this production. . . . the one when Mr. Granville Barker, as the boy, clung shivering and shrieking with cowardice, to the door post, at the notion of going to sea in a smack he knew to be rotten." *The Sovereign*, 30 April 1904, p. 204.
31 At the King's Hall, Covent Garden, on 31 January and 2 February.
32 At the Royal Court, 26, 27 and 28 June. Eventually, this play was largely rewritten and became *The Unicorn from the Stars* by Yeats and Lady Gregory.
33 The first on 26 April 1904.
34 See Barker, *The Exemplary Theatre* (London, 1922), pp. v–vi.
35 Purdom, p. 18, gives 1900 as the year in which Barker and Archer met.
36 17 December, 1902.
37 *The Vikings* for 30 performances from 15 April; *Much Ado* for 36 performances from 23 May; Ellen Terry as Hjordis and Beatrice.

[38] First produced at the Theatre Royal, Newcastle, 18 September 1902; at the Shaftesbury for 35 performances from 21 January 1903.

[39] The play referred to here is *A Daughter's Crime*, later retitled *Temptation*, by Russell Vaun, first produced at the New Theatre, Peckham on 1 August 1904. Wade made a hit, according to *The Era* (6 August 1904), as Lord Sefton.

[40] The repertoire of the Benson B, or North, Company during 1904–5 consisted of *Romeo and Juliet*, *The Taming of the Shrew*, *The Merry Wives of Windsor*, *As You Like It*, *The Merchant of Venice*, *Hamlet*, *Twelfth Night*, *The School for Scandal* and *She Stoops to Conquer*. There is a glimpse of Wade in the columns of The Era, whose Motherwell correspondent reported that he was "clever as Gratiano and was ably supported by Mr. Courtenay Foote as Bassanio." (*Era*, 4 March 1905.)

[41] For information about Katherine Boyce at this time, see Forrest C. Pogue, *George C. Marshall: Education of a General, 1880–1939* (New York, 1963), pp. 264–5. Her parts with the Benson company included Juliet, Katherine, Viola, and Nerissa opposite Wade's Gratiano.

[42] The company was at the Devonshire Park Theatre, Eastbourne, for the week of 8 May 1905; it did not visit Hastings.

[43] Barnes played Sir Howard Hallam. His autobiography, *Forty Years On the Stage* (London, 1914) offers some comments on the production and Ellen Terry, pp. 278–280.

[44] Barker had joined the Fabian Society in 1901 and was a member of its executive from 1907 until 1911.

[45] Hankin, *Dramatic Sequels* (London, 1901); reprinted in 1925 with an introduction by Hebert Farjeon.

[46] *The Cassilis Engagement* at the Imperial Theatre, 10 and 11 February 1907; and *The Last of the De Mullins* at the Haymarket, 6 and 7 December 1908.

[47] Hankin committed suicide on 15 June 1909. Many years later Shaw wrote of Hankin: "One of the masters of comedy among my playwright colleagues drowned himself because he thought he was going his father's way like Oswald Alving." (*Back to Methuselah*, revised edition, 1945, p. 300).

[48] In fact a note in the programme gave credit to Carfax and Co. Ltd. for the arrangement of the picture gallery. (Mander and Mitchenson, *Theatrical Companion to Shaw*, (London, 1955) p. 113). Beerbohm's review, "Mr. Shaw's Roderick Hudson," appeared in *The Saturday Review*, 24 November 1906, and was reprinted in *Around Theatres* (London, 1924).

[49] *The Reformer* was by Cyril Harcourt, *nom de plume* of Cyril Perkins.

[50] Barker was hired to replace Albert Gran in *Magda* in March 1900, but Gran was brought back into the cast and Barker dismissed. He therefore claimed that according to theatrical custom he was entitled to his salary for the run of the play. He won the court action and was awarded £60. Purdom, p. 9.

[51] Hearn played Judge Brack. Among his other parts at the Court were Roebuck Ramsden, Bohun in *You Never Can Tell*, Cutler Walpole in *The Doctor's Dilemma* and John Borthwick, M.P. in Galsworthy's *Silver Box*.

[52] In connection with Mrs. Campbell's performances in Yeats's *Deirdre of the Sorrows* in October and November of 1908. See p. 26.

[53] *Paola and Francesca* had opened on 6 March and ran until 5 July. In October 1902 Elizabeth Robins appeared as Alice Manisty in thirteen matinee performances of Mrs. Humphrey Ward's *Eleanor*, one of which Wade saw; see p. 7. These were her last appearances.

[54] Barker went to New York with William Archer immediately after the Savoy season of 1907–1908.

[55] See Shaw to Barker, 24 May 1907. *Collected Letters, 1898–1910*, pp. 689–692.

[56] *The Path to Rome* was published in April 1902. Charles Gore was the first bishop of the new see of Birmingham from 1905 to 1911, and then of Oxford. Barker later thought him a possible ally in the campaign against the censorship when that issue was due to be debated in the House of Lords in 1912. See Purdom, p. 137.

[57] In Winifred Loraine, *Robert Loraine* (London, 1938), p. 89.

[58] This was not Shaw's stage direction, though it is how Barker had made up for the part, looking like a young Bernard Shaw. There are photographs showing Loraine as Tanner in Mander and Mitchenson, pp. 90, 91, 93.

[59] The final performance was on 28 June 1907.

[60] The dinner was held on 7 July 1907. The proceedings were recorded in the Souvenir Book of the occasion, and reprinted in *The Shaw Review*, vol. II. no. 8 (May, 1959), pp. 17–34, and again as an appendix to the edition of Desmond MacCarthy's *The Court Theatre*, edited by Stanley

Weintraub and published as no. 6 in the Books of the Theatre Series sponsored by the American Educational Theatre Association (Coral Gables, Fla., 1966).

[61] It was, in 1966. See previous note.

[62] The Savoy held 986 as against 642 at the Court.

[63] Wade played Dick Morton. Dolly Minto was replaced by Phyllis Embury as Joy.

[64] See Shaw's letters to Lena Ashwell, 4 and 7 November 1907, in *Collected Letters, 1898–1910*, pp. 718–720. Eadie, who played Lord Charles Catelupe, was not replaced.

[65] Aimée de Burgh played Mrs. Spencer, Wade the footman.

[66] John Drinkwater.

[67] What he actually wrote was: "When you say you have corrected Ann Leete and Voysey for the press, I hope you don't imply that you are going to publish them without Waste. That would be a fatal mistake—just the sort of hopeless monstrous error that would appeal to a publisher. Get Waste ready as fast as you can: the three plays must be published in one volume, with preface and portrait, before next spring." Shaw to Barker, 25 August 1908. See Purdom (ed.) *Bernard Shaw's Letters to Granville Barker* (London, 1957), p. 136.

[68] The firm of Sidgwick and Jackson was founded in 1908.

[69] Wells was to have played Gilbert Wedgecroft. Clemence Housman played Miss Trebell; her name is missing from the playbill reproduced in Purdom, p. 76.

[70] 1879–1929, the author of *David Ballard*, which had been produced by the Stage Society in June 1907.

[71] *Daily Mail*, 30 January 1908.

[72] See Shaw to Barker, 17 November 1907, *Collected Letters, 1898–1910*, pp. 724–5.

[73] See the account in Swears' autobiography, *When All's Said and Done* (London, 1937), ch. vii.

[74] Vedrenne was not convinced. See the excerpts from letters by Shaw to him quoted in Purdom, p. 84.

[75] December 1908; reprinted in *A Motley* (London, 1910).

[76] There were two tours, one of *You Never Can Tell*, the other, led by Barker, comprising both *Arms and the Man* and *Man and Superman*. The curtain-raiser in which Wade appeared was *The Convict on the Hearth* by Frederick Fenn.

[77] Symons was removed to Brooke House, Upper Clapton Road, following his escape from Beacon Court, Crowsborough. On arrival at Brooke House, on 2 November 1908, he was officially certified insane. See Roger Lhombreaud, *Arthur Symons* (London, 1963), pp. 244–247.

[78] See also Shaw to Wade, 24 November 1908, in *Collected Letters*, 1898–1910, pp. 820–1; and Purdom, p. 87.

[79] Wade's reference here is to Congreve's *The Double Dealer*, which he produced for the Stage Society at the Queen's Theatre on 14 and 15 May 1916.

[80] Yeats' sister, Elizabeth, had founded the Dun Emer Press in 1903. It became the Cuala Press in 1908.

[81] Calderon's translation of *The Seagull* was used for the first production of a Chekhov play in Britain, at the Royalty Theatre, Glasgow, 2 November 1909.

[82] This was the Stage Society's fiftieth production, given at the Aldwych Theatre on 2 and 3 May 1909; Wade played Edward Brindley.

[83] At the Shaftesbury Theatre, 26 and 27 January 1908.

[84] *The Great Adventure* began its run at the Kingsway Theatre on 25 March 1913. Wade was by this time again working as a play-reader for Barker who had leased both the Kingsway and the Little Theatre.

[85] Conal O'Riordan was known as Norreys Connell.

[86] Denis Donoghue has noted that Wade inserted a loose leaf in Yeats's Journal recalling this episode, because the last line of the poem, to AE, differed from both the version published later and the version in the journal. Wade wrote, "W.B.Y. recited this to me at lunch in the Queen's Restaurant, Sloane Square, I think in the summer of 1909. The last line then ran: 'But tell me—does the wild dog praise his fleas.'" W. B. Yeats, *Memoirs*, edited by Denis Donoghue (London, 1972), p. 222.

[87] The triple-bill consisted of Meredith's *The Sentimentalists*, produced by Barker and sandwiched between Barrie's *Old Friends* and *The Twelve-Pound Look*, both produced by Boucicault.

[88] See also Leon Edel's comments in his edition of *The Complete Plays of Henry James* (London, 1949), which includes some further remarks by Wade.

[89] *The Green Helmet*, in which Wade played Laegaire, opened at the Court on 22 June 1910.

[90] Adapted by Cosmo Hamilton from *Le Costaud des Epinettes* by Tristan Bernard and Alfred Athis, it ran from September 6–23, 1910.

[91] Her real name was Theresa Cabre. She first attracted attention in June 1913 at the London Hippodrome in *Hello Ragtime!* followed by *Hello Tango!* at the same theatre. In August 1914 she was in *Not Likely!* at the Alhambra, and then at the Palace, in September 1915, in *Bric-à-Brac* and, in November 1916, in *Vanity Fair*.

[92] Probably F. Anstey's *Vice Versa*, adapted from his novel of the same name, and at the Comedy from 10 November 1910.

[93] *The Witch* was staged by Granville Barker for Lillah McCarthy, who played Anne Pedersen, that part having been played by Madge McIntosh when the play had its first British production at Glasgow the previous year. It was revived by Nancy Price at the Little Theatre in 1933, and at the Arts in 1944. It formed the basis of Carl Dreyer's 1943 film, *Day of Wrath*.

[94] At the Court, 21 February 1911.

[95] He played Flawner Bannel in *Fanny's First Play*.

[96] *Times*, 14 February 1912.

[97] The first of these at the Kingsway on 22 February. Wade played Ned Pearn.

[98] 19 March 1912.

[99] 7 May 1912.

[100] 7 September 1912.

[101] 21 September 1912.

[102] A condensed version of *Sumurun* had been produced at the Coliseum on 3 January 1911, and revived there, 21 August 1911, but a run of the full version had played at the Savoy from 5 October to 4 November 1911.

[103] See Appendix, pp. 37–38.

[104] Reprinted in Mander & Mitchenson, pp. 95–6.

[105] Newman Flower (ed.) *The Journal of Arnold Bennett, 1911–1921* (London, 1932) p. 59.

[106] Leo G. Sera, *On the Tracks of Life; the immorality of morality*, translated by J. M. Kennedy with an introduction by Dr. Oscar Levy (London, 1909). Levy was the editor of the English translation of the Works of Nietzsche.

[107] She died at the age of 49, on 11 November 1931. She did in fact return to the legitimate stage late in her career when she played Gladys in *Double Dan*, by Edgar Wallace, at the Savoy in May 1927.

[108] *Journals of Arnold Bennett, 1911–1921*, p. 76.

[109] Six different bills in repertory for a three week period, 1–20 December 1913.

[110] See Purdom, pp. 147–8.

[111] See also Denis Mackail, *The Story of J. M. B.* (London, 1941) pp. 468–470.

[112] Christopher Hassall, *Edward Marsh* (London, 1959), p. 384.

[113] Wade (ed.), *The Letters of W. B. Yeats* (London, 1954), p. 607.

[114] Marshall, *The Other Theatre* (London, 1947) pp. 77–78.

[115] Raymond Massey, *A Hundred Different Lives* (Toronto, 1979), p. 46.

[116] *Ibid.*, p. 47.

[117] *Ibid.*, p. 58.

[118] Quoted in Betty Lee, *Love and Whisky: the Story of the Dominion Drama Festival* (Toronto, 1973), p. 219.

[119] Above, p. 9.

[120] Leon Edel (ed.), *The Complete Plays of Henry James* (London, 1949), p. 763.

[121] Leon Edel and Dan. H. Laurence, *A Bibliography of Henry James* (London, 1961), p. 20.

[122] Henry James, *The Scenic Art*, (London, 1949), p. vi.

[123] *Times*, 15 July 1955.

[124] *Times*, 27 July 1955.

[125] *Complete Plays of Henry James*, p. 402.

Allan Wade—A Personal Memory
by Freda Gaye

I first met Allan Wade in 1922 following the Stage Society production of C. K. Munro's play *The Rumour* at the Aldwych Theatre. He had directed the play. Sadly, I cannot now recollect more of the circumstances, but I remember well his friendliness and the kind indulgence of my years as he stood talking to the author and his friends. I also remember sensing clearly from their conversation something of the kind of theatre in which I hoped one day to have a small part.

In looking back over more than thirty years of friendship, I am gratefully aware of his influence. Through his respect for the theatre he gave me—quite unwittingly—a perspective and values that I still hold.

I was indeed fortunate when he invited me to walk-on in three of his last Phoenix Society productions. It was my first professional appearance, and I remember being impressed by the discipline of our rehearsals in spite of a cast who came and went according to their existing West End commitments. This put a strain on their fellow players, but I never recall Allan losing his authority, his good humour, or his calm. He was respected by the actors for his scholarship, and loved for his gift of making a company happy. Athene Seyler, one of his early players has said of him: "Allan brought them together." At some point around this time, he discovered that we both enjoyed swimming. Thereafter, he would invite as many actors with sufficient energy left after rehearsal to join him in the Public Swimming Bath at Westminster.

Following his successful production of *The Rumour* at the Court Theatre in 1929, when his handling of the crowd scenes and marshalling of the soldiers on that small stage, with its limited wing space was a considerable challenge, his wife, Margot Sieveking, the actress, told me that Allan had been invited to accept the appointment of director at the Old Vic, but had declined it cheerfully on the grounds that "I could never have coped with Lillian Baylis."

During the next ten years, our meetings were less frequent, due to our separate engagements, but our reunions were always enthusiastic.

Allan spent, as he had always done, most of his free time in the Reading Room of the British Museum, where he was absorbed in his own research. This came as no surprise to his friends, who had known of his first passion for literature. It was now becoming his predominant interest. If I felt at this time a loosening of his theatre bonds, I never heard him refer to it. Nor did I question it, since he was clearly content. I believe that what may have appeared as lack of personal ambition was due to the disappearance of his early hopes for a progressive English theatre with a serious standard. Promotion for the idea of a National Theatre had been stirring for some years before Granville Barker and William Archer had produced their comprehensive *Schemes and Estimates for a National Theatre* in 1907; a committee had been formed and money subscribed, but the subsequent fortunes of two world wars were to put the project into cold storage for the next half century, and Allan Wade did not live to see it realized. There was also the shock following the departure of Granville Barker from the London theatre. Allan was not alone in the general disillusionment felt by all Barker's admirers, as for eight years he had worked continuously with his director, as actor, as secretary, as play-reader, and as manager; and in 1908 in Dublin, he remained to care for Barker in his serious illness, interrupting his own tour to do so. There is testimony in a letter from Bernard Shaw pointing out how indispensable Allan had become at this time, when he paid tribute to the risk and extent of his services, "completely outside your contract and inside your own goodwill."[1]

Finally there was the end of the Stage Society. Allan Wade had been associated with it since its inception, and had served as part-time secretary, as member of the Executive Committee, and had directed fourteen of its plays. Moreover he had enjoyed the stimulation and rich satisfaction of contributing to a chapter of theatre history at a time of particular significance.

The London scene had little to offer him at this time, and he and Margot Wade spent much of their time in the South of France where he continued the work of assembling his collection of Henry James papers on the drama. We met just once in 1939 in Menton, where I found them both busy and happy. In two years they were back in England, making their home in Boscastle in Cornwall, which had been Allan's birthplace.

It is, I think typical of Allan that the reason given for his original intention for the Henry James Notes and Papers was not one of personal ambition, but a "whim born of a desire to have on his own shelves these papers assembled so that they could be read and reread".[2]

It is none the less gratifying to his friends to know that not long before he died—after the publication of his Yeats Bibliography—Margot Wade spoke affectionately of Allan's response to a glowing review of the book. He looked at her happily and said: "I have become a Literary Gent!"

His qualities remain vivid and strong. A clear intellect, warmly affectionate, with an integrity of such conviction that he did not bother to argue, and a laughter that came frequently and with refreshing ease. But as I remember him now, I find that the quality that remains clearly, is one of content.

---

[1] *Collected Letters of Bernard Shaw (1898–1910)*, edited by Dan H. Laurence, 1972.
[2] *The Scenic Art—Henry James (1872–1901)*, edited by Allan Wade, 1949, from the Foreword by Leon Edel.

Index

Achurch, Janet   4, 5
Acis and Galatea   6, 7, 37
actor-managers   1
Adelphi Theatre   2, 26
Admirable Bashville, The   42
Admirable Crichton, The   7
Admiral Guinea   8
Adored One, The   35
Aglavaine and Selysette   10
Agnes Colander   8
Ainley, Henry   21, 32, 33, 35, 39, *pl.5*
Alchemist, The   40
Alexander, George   1, 27
All for Love   40
Allgood, Sara   28, 29
American Tragedy, An   41
Anatol   30
Andrews, Alan   ix, xiii–xv
Androcles and the Lion   34, 39
Archer, William   8, 19, 20, 25, 26, 27, 35
Arizona   2
Arms and the Man   3, 19, 21, 23, 24, 41
Arts Theatre   42
Ashwell, Lena   18, 26, 40
Asquith, Herbert   35
At Mrs Beam's   42
At the Hawk's Well   39
Attila   2
Au Petit Bonheur   39
Avenue Theatre   3, 19
Aylwin, Jean   35

Barker, H. Granville   3–8 *passim*, 10–21
  passim, 23–35 *passim*, 37–8, 39, 42; Prefaces
  to Shakespeare 34
Barnes, J.H.   11, 45(n43)
Barrie, J.M.   2, 27–8, 31, 35
Barton, Mary   12
Becky Sharp   3–4
Beerbohm, Max   7, 14, 27, 43
Bennett, Arnold   26, 33, 34
Benson's North company   9, 10, 45(n40)
Bernhardt, Sarah   1
Bethlehem   9
Beyond the Horizon   41
Bishop, Gwendolen   6
Bluestone Quarry, The   42
Bolt from the Blue, A   30
Boucicault, Dion   28, 29–30, 35, 39
Bourchier, Arthur   1
Bowyer, Arthur   20
Boyce, Katherine   9, 10, 42, 45(n41)
Bradfield College Greek Theatre   31
Brothers Karamazov, The   39
Brough, Fanny   5, 21
Browne, Graham   35

Bryant, Charles   29
"Bull-dog Breed, The"   35
Bullen, A.H.   17, 22, 23, 24
Burgh, Aimée de   19

Caesar and Cleopatra   18
Calderon, George   26
Campbell, Mrs Patrick   1, 15, 25, 26–7
Campden Wonder, The   14
Canada: Dominion Drama Festival   42
Canary, The   15
Candida   3, 4, 8, 10
Cannan, Gilbert   19, 20
Captain Brassbound's Conversion   3, 11
Carr, George   40, 41
Carson, Murray   3, 18
Carton, R.C.   2
Case of Rebellious Susan, The   3
Casson, Lewis   12
censorship   5, 7, 9, 18–19, 27 (Royal
  Commission), 28, 31, 45(n56)
Chains   29
Chambers, Haddon   2
Charity that Began at Home, The   13–14
Charrington, Charles   4
Chesterton, G.K.   27, 35
Chinese Lantern, The   21
Claire, Ina   35
Cloudy with Showers   41
Coffin, Hayden   32
Comedy Theatre   3
Coming of Peace, The   4
Common People   41
Comtesse Mitzi   41
Coquelin   1
Coronet Theatre   6
Country Wife, The   40, 41
Court Theatre   8, 10–17 *passim*, 25, 29, 30
Craig, E. Gordon   6, 7, 9, 37
Craig, Edith   40, 42
Crane, Walter   4
Creditors, The   42
Cupid and Common Sense   26

Dallas, Irene   38
Daughter's Crime, A   45(n39) *ref. back to* 9
Davies, H.H.   2
Death of Tintagiles, The   4, 34
Deirdre   25, 29
Deslys, Gaby   35
Devil's Disciple, The   3, 18, 19
Diaghilev, Serge   31
Dictator, The   42
Dido and Aeneas   6
Digges, Dudley   29
Doctor's Dilemma, The   14, 34

Double Dealer, The 39
Double Game, The 31
Drinkwater, A.E. 19, 30, 35
Drinkwater, John 13
Drury Lane Theatre 2, 11
Dublin 23–5; Abbey Theatre 24–5, 28, 29;
  Company at Court Theatre 26, 29
Duchess of Malfi, The 40
Duke of York's Theatre 25–6, 28, 30
Dukes, Ashley 39, 40
Dulac, Edmund 39
Du Maurier, Gerald 29, 35
Duse, Eleonora 1

Eadie, Dennis 13, 18, 26, 30, 39
Edel, Leon 42, 43
Edwardes, George 1, 27
Eldest Son, The 33
Eleanor 7, 44(n26)
Elizabeth Cooper 39
Embassy Theatre 41
Esther Waters 39
Evans, Edith 40
Everyman Theatre 40, 41

Fanny's First Play 30, 31, 33, 39
Faustus 40
First Mrs Fraser, The 41
Fletcher, Constance Kyrle ix, xi
For Sword or Song 9
Forbes-Robertson, Johnston 1, 7, 18
Fountain, The 26
Fourberies de Scapin, Les 25
Fraser, Winifred 6
Frohman, Charles 25–6, 28, 29

Galsworthy, John 12, 13, 14, 19, 20, 23, 27, 31
Gaye, Freda ix, xiii, 48–9
General Strike 41
Gentleman Dancing Master, The 40
Gerard, Theodora 30, 47(n91)
Getting Married 21
Gielgud, John 40
Gift Horse, The 41
Gill, Eric and Macdonald 28
Gillette, William 1
Good Hope, The 8, 44(n30)
Granier, Jeanne 1
Grant, Duncan, designer 42
Great Adventure, The 26, 33, *pl.8*
Great Queen St Theatre 6, 25
Green Cockatoo, The 39
Green Helmet, The 29
Gregory, Lady 24–8 *passim*
Grierson's War 8
Griffith, Troyte, designer 18
Gwenn, Edmund 10, 12, 35

Hading, Jane 1
Hallard, C.M. 6, 26
Hampstead Conservatoire 6
Hankin, St John 3, 12, 13, 14, 19, 20, 45(n47)
Hannen, Nicholas 41

Hare, John 1, 29
Harlequinade 34
Hart-Davis, Rupert ix, xiii, 42, 43
Harvey, John Martin 1
Hawtrey, Charles 26
Haymarket Theatre 1, 3, 21, 26
Hearn, James 15, 45(n51)
Hedda Gabler 15
Heggie, O.P. 34, 35
Helena's Path 29
Hell Bent for Heaven 41
Herod 2
Hignett, H.R. 14
Hippolytus 8, 10
His Majesty's Theatre 1, 2
Holloway, Balliol 40
House of Usna, The 4
Housman, Laurence 12, 21, 27; and
  Clemence 19, 20
Howard de Walden, Lord 35

Ibsen, Henrik 2–3
Image, The 29
Imperial Theatre 9, 18
In the Zone 40
*Interesses Creados, Los (The Bias of the
  World)* 39
Interior 4
Intermezzo 42
Iphigenia in Tauris 31
Irving, Henry 1, 3
Irving, Laurence 15, 26
Ito, Michio 39

James, Henry 19, 31, 42–3
Jazz Patterns 41
Jeans, Isabel 40, 41
Jew of Malta, The 40
John Bull's Other Island 10, 11, 12, 33
John Gabriel Borkman 8
Jones, Henry Arthur 2, 3, 7
Jones, Robert E., designer 39
Joy 17
Justice 28, 29

Kahn, Otto 15, 16
Kendals, the 1
Kennedy, W.S. 40
Kerr, Fred 11
Kerrigan, J.M. 29
King Lear 26
Kingsway Theatre 31, 33, 39, 42
Knoblock, Edward 4

Lablache, Luigi 18
Lambourn, Amy 12
Land of Heart's Desire, The 42
Lang, Matheson 18
Last Enemy, The 41
Lawrence, W.J. 25
League of Youth, The 4
Leblanc, Georgette 7
Lewis, Eric 14

Literary Theatre Society   6
Little Eyolf   8
Little Theatre   30, 31, 39
Lloyd, Frederick   12, 24
Lloyd George, David   35
Lohr, Marie   35
London Public Morality Council   41
Loraine, Robert   15, 16, 21, 41
Love for Love   39, 40
Lowe, Trevor   12
Lugné-Poë, Aurélien   7

Macbeth   34–5
MacCarthy, Desmond   16, 17
McCarthy, Lillah   10, 20, 32, 34, 35, 39, 47(n93), *pl.6*
MacDermott, Norman   40
McEvoy, Charles   19
Machine Infernale, La   42
McIntosh, Madge   47(n93), *pl.2*
McKinnel, Norman   14, 18, 26
Madras House, The   11, 29
Maid's Tragedy, The   40
Major Barbara   10
Man and Superman   10, 15, 16, 21, 24
Man of Destiny, The   3, 16
Man of Honour, A   8
Man who Married a Dumb Wife, The   39
Many Waters   41
Mariage Forcé, Le   34
Mariana   8
Marrying of Ann Leete, The   5–6, 10, 19
Marsh, Edward   39
Marshall, Norman   40
Masefield, John   12, 23–4, 31
Masque of Love   6, 7
Massey, Raymond   40, 41
Massingham, H.W.   8
Master Builder, The   30
Matthews, A.E.   13
Maude, Cyril   1, 3
Maugham, Somerset   8
Medea   18
Mental Athletes, The   42
Merchant of Venice, The   45(n40)
Middle Watch, The   41
Midsummer Night's Dream, A   34, *pl.7*
Minto, Dorothy   12, 17
Miracle, A
Misalliance   29
Monna Vanna   7
Moore, George   24, 31
Morley, Malcolm   40
Mr Pepys   41
Mrs Warren's Profession   5, *pl.2*
Much Ado about Nothing   9
Munro, C.K.   39
Murray, Gilbert   12, 19, 20

National Theatre project   8, 48
Neilson, Julia   1
Nelson Touch, The   41
Nesbitt, Cathleen   40

Nethersole, Olga   4
New Century Theatre   8
New Lyric Club   5

O'Donovan, Fred   29
"One Night"   35
O'Neill, Maire   29
O'Neill, Mollie   29
O'Riordan, Conal   26–7
Orphan, The   40
Othello   7
Our Visitor to "Work-a-Day"   6
Outcry, The   28, 29, 42
Owen, Reginald   30
Oxford Music Hall, Marylebone   1
Oxford Playhouse   42

Page, Norman   12, 26
Palace Theatre   30
Paolo and Francesca   2, 15
Passion, Poison and Petrifaction   10
Pavilion Theatre   1
Persians   6
Peter Pan   30
Philanderer, The   14
Philanthropists, The   8
Philbrick, Norman   xi
Phillips, Stephen   2
Phoenix Society   40, 42, 48
Pinero, A.W.   2, 13, 27, 31
Playboy of the Western World, The   25, 29
Playfair, Nigel   31
Pleasure Garden, The   42
Ponsonby, Magdalen   20
Potiphar's Wife   41
Pretenders, The   26
Progress   42
Prunella   10, 11, 16, 29
Purcell Operatic Society   6

Queen's Theatre   18, 19, 21

Raleigh   42
Raleigh, Cecil   2
Ranalow, Frederick   41
Rat Trap, The   41
Raymond Mander and Joe Mitchenson Theatre Collection: *pls 3, 4, 5, 6, 8*
Reading, Jack   xiii
Reeves, Mrs W.P.   20
Reformer, The   14
Regent's Park, booth in   10
Reinhardt, Max   32, 37
Réjane   1
Reprobate, The   41, 43
Return of the Prodigal, The   13, 14, 15
Richards, Grant   4, 5
Ricketts, Charles   6, 16, 20, 26, 34
Robertson, Graham   7
Robins, Elizabeth   8, 15, 31, 45(n53)
Robinson, F. Cayley, designer   18
Rococo   30, 31
Ross, Robert   14

Rosy Rapture 35
Royalty Theatre 4, 5, 21, 39, 41
Rumour, The 42, 48
Rutherston (*or* Rothenstein), Albert,
    designer 32, 34, 37

St James's Theatre 1, 2, 15, 34
St Martin's Theatre 41
Sapho (Daudet) 4, 44(n8)
Savoy Theatre 16–21 *passim*, 32, 34, 35, 37–8
Secret Woman, The 31
Sentimentalists, The 28, 31
Seyler, Athene 40, 41, 48
Shakespeare Head Press 22–3
Sharp, William 4
Shaw, G.B. 3, 4, 5, 7, 10–19 *passim*, 21, 24, 25,
    27, 30, 31, 34, 35, 41, 46(n67), 48
Shaw, Martin 6
Shewing-up of Blanco Posnet, The 28
Sidgwick, Frank 16, 17, 19, 22
Sieveking, Margot (Mrs Wade) 41, 48, 49
Silver Box, The 12, 13, 34
Sime, S.H., designer 26
Sinclair, Arthur 29
Sinclair family: their portable theatre 22–3
Six Characters in Search of an Author 42
Speaight, George ix
Stage Society 3, 4, 7, 8, 13, 14, 18, 19, 26, 35,
    36, 39–42 *passim*, 48
Stephens, Yorke 4
Strife 17, 25
Summers, Montague 40, 42
Sumurun 32
Sutro, Alfred 2, 7–8, 31
Swears, Herbert 21
Swinley, Ion 40
Symons, Arthur 5, 7, 23–4, *pl.4*

"Taming a Tiger" 35
Tearle, Godfrey 35
Tempest, Marie 3, 35
Terriss, William 3
Terry, Ellen 3, 11, 44(n37), 45(n43)
Terry, Fred 1, 9
Terry's Theatre 3
Theatre Museum 20, *pls 2, 7*
Thesiger, Ernest 40
Thomas, Berte 6
Thompson 26
Thompson, Hazel 12
Thorndike, Sybil 40
Tinney, Frank 35
Tivoli Music Hall 1
Tragedy of Nan, The 21, 30, 31, 34
Tree, Beerbohm 1, 16, 27
Trelawney of the "Wells" 29
Trench, Herbert 26
Twelfth Night 32, *pl.5*
Twelve Pound Look, The 29, 31
Twentieth Century Theatre 7, 44(n22)
Two Mr Wetherbys, The 13

Ulysses 2
Uncle Vanya 39

Vanbrugh, Irene 29, 30, 35
Vanbrugh, Violet 1
Vedrenne, J.E. 12, 16–21 *passim*, 24, 39, *pl.3*
Vedrenne-Barker management: at Court
    Theatre 10–16; at Savoy 17–21
Venice Preserv'd 40
Veronica 42
Vezin, Hermann 4
Vibart, Henry 35
Victoria Hall, Bayswater 7, 44(n22)
Vikings, The 9
Volpone 40
Votes for Women! 15
Voysey Inheritance, The 8, 10–11, 19, 31, 33,
    37

Wade, Allan: sketch *pl. 1*: brief survey of life
    xiii–xiv; explores London theatres 1–9; joins
    Stage Society 5; in Benson North company
    9–10; in Vedrenne-Barker management 11—;
    to Dublin 23–5; and Abbey Players in London
    25—; and Frohman Repertory 28—; and
    Barker's further ventures 32—; as Stage
    Society Secretary 35—; and Phoenix Society
    40—; literary work 10, 22–3, 42–3; a personal
    memory 48–9
Wade, Mrs Allan *see* Sieveking
Wade, Mrs Peggy ix, *pl.1*
Wade, Rev. Stephen xiii
Wallack's Theatre 39
Wanderers 39
Waste 15, 18, 19, 20
Weather Hen, The 3, 6
Welch, James 4
Wells, H.G. 19, 20, 31
What the Public Wants 26
Whelan, Frederick 4, 27, 35
"When the Kye Comes Home" 35
Where there is Nothing 8
White Chateau, The 41
White Devil, The 42
"Why? A Conundrum" 35
Widowers' Houses 3, 41
Wild Duck, The 34
Wilde, Oscar: Letters 43
Wilkinson, Norman, designer 32, 34, 37, 39,
    40
Winter's Tale, The 32, 37–8, *pl.6*
Witch, The 30, 34, 47(n93)
Witch of Edmonton, The 40
Wyndham, Charles 1, 3
Wyndham's Theatre 1, 3
Wynne, Wish 33, *pl.8*

Yacco, Sada and Kawakami 1
Yeats, W.B. 4, 7, 8, 10, 17, 22, 24–9 *passim*,
    37, 42, 46(n86)
You Never Can Tell 3, 4, 12, 17, 23